Hear Me Cry

A Fantasy Romance Retelling of the Irish
legend of the Banshee

AMANDA J EVANS

ALSO BY AMANDA J EVANS

Finding Forever

Save Her Soul

Mermaids Shouldn't Run (A short romantic comedy story)

Mistletoe Magic (A short romantic Christmas story)

Coming Soon

The Cursed Angels

CONTENTS

DEDICATION

For Dad. Until we meet again, sleep well. .

PROLOGUE

Existing in Irish folklore for centuries, Banshee, or *bean sidhe,* means "woman of the faery". It hasn't always been my name, and I haven't always been the messenger of death. You see, I was cursed, so my mourning call now heralds death. They say love is the cure for all, but it was love that cursed me. You think you know about me, but it's time I tell the real story.

CHAPTER ONE

Border patrol was always boring. Walking up and down along the veil, eyes peeled in case any human should cross. I hated it, especially the south patrol. Nothing ever happened. To make matters worse, I was alone. No one to chat with, the rustling leaves beneath my feet the only sound. It was just me on the border of the Summer and Autumn Courts, walking between the crisp leaves and blooming flowers. I wanted to be where the action was, where the rest of the warriors were stationed. The north. It was colder and rougher terrain, but at least they saw action. I was stuck here watching the leaves fall off the trees, the large branches shielding me from the blazing sun. Nothing to look at but forest and fields of flowers. Poppies as far as the eye could see.

"Why couldn't I have been sent to the north?" I sighed as I kicked a pile of leaves. "It's not fair." I knew why. It was because I was short, slight, and female. But I could take any of the male warriors and they knew it.

I turned to march along the trail again, the sunlight bouncing off the rippling veil that kept the faery and human worlds separate. The humans couldn't see or feel the veil, but to me it looked like a pool of clear water suspended in mid-air, rippled from the breeze that blew against it. It has a bluish tint to it as well. It was about the only pleasant thing to look at. The trees lost their appeal after an hour and the poppies, if I didn't see one again for the rest of my life I wouldn't care. Who needs fields and fields of them anyway? The Summer Queen must have run out of ideas. I scoffed as I marched through the trees. *What's the point in being a trained warrior if I never see battle, never get to kill a human?*

I'd never seen a human, but I had heard the stories. Vicious beings who loved nothing better than to capture a fae and torture them to death or, worse, enslave them for eternity. I shuddered at the thought.

"Help! Help!"

The shouts echoed. I jumped, turning on my heels to see where the noise was coming from.

"Help!"

"It's coming from inside the veil," I mumbled as I raced forward. My mind conjured up images of fallen fae, my brothers, trapped and pleading for help. Instinct kicked in and I jumped through the barrier between our worlds, awakening all my senses.

My feet sank into lush green grass and I crouched low, blinking rapidly as bright sunlight assaulted my eyes. I tossed my dark curls over my shoulders and turned my head left and right, looking for the threat. It was quiet. Tall oaks trees covered the ground on both sides, a short pathway through them where the veil had spat me out. In front of me was a vast expanse of water, surrounded by hills and mountains. The grass here was greener than I'd ever seen. I pushed to my feet, looking behind me at the rippling veil. I could only see a small opening from this side, the rest hidden in the canopy of trees. No wonder no humans ever made it through to the other side.

"Help!"

I spun. The shouts came from the water. Two hands

poked up through the surface, waving frantically before they were swallowed, pulled beneath and into the darkness.

Running toward the embankment, I kicked off my shoes and plunged into the water. Fae normally weren't very good swimmers…except for me. I loved the water. It called to me on a deeper level, obeying my commands. I don't know why and no one seemed to be able to explain it either.

I opened my eyes to look through the darkness. Another of my talents. When I saw legs kicking, I forced my body in that direction. The water clung to my clothes, trying to drag me into the depths. The figure started to sink again, arms raised. I was too late.

I pushed myself as hard as I could. Grabbing a fistful of hair, I tugged upward so I could get a firm grasp on the body. I kicked my legs and we rose to the surface. My head emerged and I sucked in a deep breath, my arm secured tightly around the person's neck. We weren't too far from shore.

I pulled the body onto the grassy bank and bent over to catch my breath, refilling my lungs, coughing up the water I'd swallowed. I pushed my wet hair back off my face, forcing it behind my shoulders. The water dripped down my back as I tried to calm my breathing.

I looked down at the body. A male. His lack wet hair covered his face but I caught of glimpse of freckles across his high cheek bones. His full lips were blue. I brush the hair out of the way and gasped when I saw his ears. A human male. He was motionless.

I bent down, watching his chest for movement. Nothing.

I knelt beside him and placed my fingers on his neck. No pulse. It shouldn't have bothered me, he was human filth, but it did. He wasn't breathing. Death was taking him and I could save him. I shouldn't want to, but it felt wrong not to try, not to give him a chance to fight.

Sucking in a deep breath, I leaned over and placed my

hands over his checked shirt, pumping hard on his chest.

"Come on. Breathe."

He remained still, his body cold.

"You can't die. Not on my watch," I said through gritted teeth.

I reached forward, looking into his pale face. He looked so peaceful, so normal. Nothing like the stories I'd been told. In fact, he looked quite harmless with his rounded ears. I gasped aloud before laughing to myself.

"I've rescued a human. Me, one of the queen's guard, sworn to protect, and I've rescued a human."

The laughter died in my chest. "What do I do? Do I let him die? He's probably dead already."

I shook my head, my hands trembling. I couldn't let him die. Not like this. Battles were different. In battle, I could cut him down in an instant, but he was defenceless right now.

I leaned forward and felt for a pulse once more. I thought I felt a flutter, but it was faint.

"You can't let him die, Isla," I whispered.

I knew I'd never forgive myself if I did nothing.

Pumping his chest once more, I waited for him to cough, breathe, something. It didn't happen.

I inhaled deeply and steadied my nerves before placing my lips to his and blowing air into his lungs. My body trembled as I pulled back.

He suddenly gasped, water spluttering from his mouth. I grabbed him and rolled him onto his side so he could breathe easier. He was heavier than I expected. No sooner had I moved him than a searing pain shot through my body and I collapsed on the ground. Uncontrollable heat coursed through my veins, like fire ripping through haystacks.

I screamed and tried to fight it. He'd tricked me, poisoned me. I should have let him drown.

The pain started to recede, sweat dripping from my forehead as I brushed my dark curls hair away. My throbbing hands felt like red-hot pokers as I waved them through the air. My heart raced. Something was wrong. I felt different, changed. I ran my fingers across my face. It felt the same, strong chin, full lips, small button nose, and pointed ears. The lake danced in my vision, blurred and distorted.

"Go hálainn," the voice croaked.

I shook my head. A spell perhaps?

"Go raibh maith agat," he spoke again, but I couldn't understand it.

My hands tingled as I held them out in front of me. Veins popped out on the surface of my skin, which was red and swollen.

"What have you done to me?" I shouted as I turned to look at the human. "What poison did you use?" My voice was strained, my throat closing in as I sat up.

"Ni thigim. Are you all right?" He sat up and reached for me.

I flinched, but as soon as his fingers touched my arm, the burning stopped, my vision clearing.

"Cé tusa?"

My gaze met his and I gasped. His eyes were so blue, so mesmerising. I was trapped in them. I felt a pull inside me. It was so strong, I couldn't resist. My hand reached out to touch his face. I couldn't stop it. The moment my fingers brushed against his skin, my mind exploded. Lights danced, magic flared, and I fell backwards.

"A Cailin, an bhfuil tu go maith?"

I forced my eyes open, seeing his face hovering over mine. "I c-can't unders-stand y-you," I stuttered, trying to regain control.

"I asked if you were okay," he said, his voice like honey, soothing my body and mind.

I swallowed. "What did you do to me? What poison did you use?"

"Poison?" He shook his head. "I didn't do anything.

You saved me. You…" He paused.

My body slowly began to feel like mine again and I sat up to look more closely at this human.

"I don't understand. When I touched you, something happened. I thought you poisoned me."

"Why would I do that?" he asked, leaning toward me, my eyes focusing on his full lips.

I jerked back. He stopped. His eyes roamed my body before coming back to my face. Those blue orbs pierced mine, making me feel the pull again. The longing to touch him. It had to be magic, an entrapment spell.

"What did you say when you woke up? Did you cast a spell on me?"

"A spell?" He laughed.

"You spoke strange words."

"I spoke my language. Irish. I said you were beautiful and I thanked you for saving me. You're not from these parts, are you?"

My instincts warned me not to answer, so I pushed to my feet. "I have to go." I looked around for my shoes, spotting them near the water's edge.

"Wait," he said, grabbing my arm.

As soon as he touched me, the heat travelled throughout my body. My vision blurred, my body swaying.

"I got you," he said as he pulled me to him.

His touch felt soothing, my body melding into his. The heat intensified, and darkness took over.

***

My senses returned, the warmth of my blanket snug around me. *Pure bliss.*

When my blanket moved, I tensed. Memories returned, and I forced my eyes open. He watched me, smiling. He was the blanket I'd felt so safe under. My head rested against his stomach as I lay across his legs.

"You okay?" he asked, watching me intently.

"What happened?"

"I don't know. You were about to leave, then passed out in my arms. I've been waiting for you to wake up. Felt like you had a fever."

"Oh." The memories came back. Saving his life, being poisoned. And he was human.

I started to sit up, immediately regretting it. Cold seeped through my veins and my body shook. When he pulled me back down, the cold vanished, replaced with that familiar warmth and comfort. I felt safe.

"What's wrong with me?" I whispered, trying to discern what was really going on. Was it a trap? Had he really poisoned me?

"There's nothing wrong with you. You're the most beautiful woman I've ever seen."

When I frowned, he leaned in closer, his stomach brushing against the side of my cheek. "What's the matter?"

"I'm not a woman."

"You could have fooled me," he laughed, his stomach muscles clenching against my face.

My body reacted, heat pulsing through my veins. All I wanted to do was snuggle against him, get as close as I could.

"I'm not a human woman," I sighed. "I'm fae."

"Well, then, you're the most beautiful fae woman I've ever seen."

His eyes sparkled as his mouth twitched, lips parted. What I wouldn't give to feel them against mine, on my bare skin.

I shook my head. *What's wrong with me?* I needed to move, get away from here. I started to sit up again. This time, he helped me.

"Are you sick?"

"I don't know what's wrong with me. My body feels like it's on fire. Are you sure you didn't poison me?"

"I'm sure," he said, placing his hand against my forehead.

A sigh escaped my mouth and I leaned into his touch. I needed it, wanted it. My eyes found his, entrancing me. I saw myself reflected in them, felt myself moving forward, then my lips were on his, ravaging his mouth. He tasted like heaven. I moaned loudly as I climbed onto his lap, wrapping my arms around his neck. I wanted more. It was all I could think of. As his tongue traced my bottom lip, I opened for him. Our tongues danced and explored. I could do this forever.

A slow burn began to flow down my arm, tingling before igniting my body. I pulled back and looked down. Black lines had formed circles, stopping just before the tips of my fingers.

"Runes," I gasped, realizing what was happening. "The mating bond." I jumped up, waving my arm through the air. "This can't be happening. It's not possible. It's not!" Tears started to form.

He stood and grabbed my shoulders, turning me to him. "What's wrong? Talk to me."

"But you're human," I sobbed. "It can't happen."

"What can't happen? I don't understand."

When the burning stopped, I pulled away. I looked down at my arm and there it was, clear for everyone to see.

The mating runes. The bond had been formed. Black swirls covered the length of my arm, ending with a half-finished infinity symbol at my fingers. I rubbed at it until my skin was raw, but it was no use.

"What is that?" he asked, brows furrowed.

"The end of my life," I sobbed.

"You're dying?!"

"I may as well be," I said, lifting my gaze to his. That was a big mistake.

As soon as our eyes met, I had an uncontrollable urge to reach out and touch him. My hand moved of its own accord, reaching for his face. He watched, unmoving. I managed to pull back at the last second and lowered my gaze. Pain ripped through my body and I bent over, clutching my stomach.

"Tell me what to do. How can I help?"

I heard the fear in his voice, but I couldn't look up. I couldn't risk it. When he touched my shoulder, the pain vanished. My head jerked up in shock, my eyes locked on his once more. Heat seeped into my body, followed by lust. Overwhelming lust.

"Please, don't touch me," I managed to choke out as I fought with myself.

"Sorry." He stepped back.

I heard the sadness in his voice as my body shook and the pain reignited.

"I have to go. I have to—"

He grabbed me and pulled me to him. "I can't let you leave me. I don't know why, but I can't," he panted, fear evident in his voice.

I was bound to this human...mind, body, and

soul…for eternity. I wanted to scream, to run, but in his arms, all I felt was pure bliss.

"What's happening to me?" he whispered as his hands caressed my back, my body reacting to every stroke.

"It's the mating bond. It has joined us. I don't know how."

"What's your name?" he whispered against my ear. His lips brushed against the side of my cheek.

"Isla," I groaned, my body betraying me.

"I'm Sean," he said before capturing my mouth in the most passionate, demanding kiss I'd ever experienced.

My mouth opened for him, my hands ripping at his clothes. I wanted to feel his skin, explore his body, join with him. I moaned into his mouth as I pulled him closer, my body pressed against his. His erection swelled in his pants.

You must stop. You can't do this. The bond is wrong, unnatural, a mistake. Get home. The queen will know what to do.

My mind fought with my body, instinct against will. Eventually, I managed to pull away. My breathing was rapid as I moved my gaze to the ground. Sean stepped toward me, but I held up my hand to stop him.

"You can't touch me," I said. "I have to get home, get this fixed. It's wrong, unnatural. Fae and human don't bond."

"Isla, please…"

"No," I said, the pain beginning once more. "Let me go. I'll fix this, then you'll see."

"But I don't *want* you to go. Something inside is telling me not to let you leave. That you're mine. Is that this bond you keep speaking of?"

"Yes," I gasped as another wave of pain washed over

me. "I have to go before it's too late."

Not giving him the chance to answer, I turned and ran, pumping my legs as fast as possible until I crossed the veil. Once through, I stopped. The pain had lessened, but the longing, the feeling of loss, overwhelmed me. I looked down at my hand, seeing the black, swirling runes still there. I took a deep breath and fought the urge to turn around, race back to him and into his arms. I remembered the feeling of his comforting touch. The softness of his lips. The passion ignited from the taste of his tongue. My body heating in anticipation as lust rolled through me.

"You have to fight it. Get home. Get it fixed," I mumbled. I wanted him so much. Wanted to feel his skin on mine, feel him inside me. "Fight!" I willed myself to listen.

Home… I had to get home and have the bond undone before it was too late. If I gave in to temptation, joined with Sean, all would be lost.

CHAPTER TWO

Pushing through the doors of the Summer Court, I finally allowed my legs to give way. Pain came in waves, sweat dripping from my body, but I'd finally made it home.

"Isla?" Morgan gasped as hands reached under my arms to help me to my feet.

I glanced up at the warriors, grateful for their assistance as they helped me move forward.

"What happened?" she asked, standing from her throne.

I had no words. Instead, I extended my arm. I watched as recognition of the bond spread across her face and she smiled.

"That's wonderful, Isla. Where is the lucky one?"

Tears streamed down my face as I struggled to get the words out. Another sharp pain buckled my body. "Human," I spluttered, watching her face fall before the pain became too much and the world slipped away.

***

My eyes felt heavy as I tried to peel them open. My body trembled, but the intense pain had subsided. I waited for my vision to clear, blinking away the sleep that had claimed me.

"She's awake. Inform the queen."

I heard the voice as I struggled to sit up. "What happened?" I asked as I took in my surroundings. This wasn't my room.

A small, stout fae girl moved to the side of the bed. "You collapsed. The queen had you brought to Isaac's chambers. He's out gathering supplies to cure you."

"The bond?" I questioned, afraid to look at my arm. She lowered her head. "It's still there?"

"Yes. But Isaac will know what to do. Can I get you anything?"

I shook my head and lay back down. I knew what happened to bonded mates who were kept apart for too long. The longing turned to torture, then madness, and finally death.

"When will he be back?" I asked.

She looked at me. "Isaac?"

"Yes."

"He won't be long. You rest now. I'll fetch some food and water."

I tried closing my eyes, but I was too anxious. I was bonded to a human. How did that happen?

The door opened and Morgan stepped inside. As she looked at me, I saw fear in her eyes. "What happened?" she asked.

"I don't know," I said, my eyes filling with tears. "I don't understand it. It's not possible."

"No, it's not." She crossed her arms over her chest. "Isla, did anything happen when the bond was formed? Did you…complete it?"

I gasped. "No. I fought it."

"Good. Isaac should be able to fix it, but you need to stay here until he does. Do you understand?"

"Yes."

"No matter what, Isla, do not leave this room."

Her serious tone struck me as odd, but I nodded. If the bond could be severed, I'd stay in the dungeons.

"I'll be back to check on you later. Get some rest. We'll have you back to normal in no time."

"Thank you," I whispered.

Morgan turned toward the door, but stopped just before she exited. "You have told me everything, haven't you, Isla?"

"Yes."

"Okay," she said, then left.

I let out a deep breath. "What a mess."

I heard my name coming from outside the door, so I sat up to listen. Morgan was talking to someone. "Find him and dispose of him quickly. I don't care how you do it. Just get it done and report back to me."

"But what of Isla?" I heard the other voice say.

"She'll be fine. The bond isn't complete. She'll survive."

There was ice in her tone. I gasped as the reality of what she said seeped in.

"Oh no, Sean," I whispered, my stomach clenching. "They're going to kill you."

My body trembled as my fear grew. Why would they kill him? I felt a tightening in my chest and my runes burned. Sean's face, lips, the feel of his body went through my mind. Without realizing, I was out of bed and pulling on my clothes. I couldn't let it happen. I wouldn't.

"Sean," I whispered as I felt the intense longing once more.

Isla?! Is that you?

His voice echoed in my mind and I shook my head. I heard him again.

Isla?

Sean? Where are you? I can hear you in my head.

Me, too. I hear you.

I looked down at my arm. The runes pulsed and swirled. *Where are you?*

I'm near the lake. I'm coming to find you.

You mustn't. They're on their way to find you and... I couldn't finish the sentence. *Please, go and hide,* I begged, tears slipping from my eyes.

I can't, he replied. *I tried. I got halfway home and my legs froze. They wouldn't work. Your face was all I could think of. As soon as I made the decision to find you, my body obeyed. I don't know what's happening to me. I can't think of anything but you, and now I'm hearing you in my head. It's not right.*

He stopped talking. I didn't know how to respond. I thought the bond hadn't affected him. He seemed fine.

Are you ill? I asked.

No. I feel stronger than I ever have. I just... I have to find you, see you.

Images of him dragging his hands through his hair in frustration danced in my mind, and my heart rate increased. Panic took over. I had to find him.

Find a place to hide. I'm coming to find you.

I'll try, he said.

Sean, don't let them find you.

I won't.

Silence resumed in my head as I circled the small room. How would I leave? I heard footsteps outside the door and jumped back into bed, pulling the covers up to my neck. I pretended to be asleep as the door opened.

"I've brought some food and a tonic to help."

It was the small girl from before. I blinked and rubbed my eyes. "Thank you," I mumbled.

"I'll just leave it here," she said, placing the tray on the bedside table. "Morgan said to make sure you drink it all. It will help with the symptoms."

I nodded and she left.

The smell of the food had my stomach grumbling, but before I took a bite, I heard voices outside my room again.

"Did you give it to her?"

Morgan.

"Yes. She was sleeping, but she woke. I told her it would help."

"Good," Morgan replied. "The potion will keep her asleep while we take care of the human. She won't wake for at least twenty-four hours."

I gasped. They were going to poison me? I looked at the tray of food. My stomach grumbled, but I ignored it. Food could wait. I had to get out of here.

I paced the length of the small room, chewing on my fingernails as I planned my escape. If they expected me to be asleep, they wouldn't be watching my room, right?

I'd never disobeyed an order before, but I'd never heard Morgan speak like that before, either. She sounded cruel, and just the thought of her words sent shivers down my spine.

I pulled open the wardrobe in the corner of the room and retrieved a cloak. I'd use the service passages. No one would pay any attention to me, and I could leave through the kitchen and out into the forest.

With my mind made up, I gripped the handle of the door, listening carefully before turning it. The hallway was empty. It was now or never.

CHAPTER THREE

It took over an hour to find Sean. I had to avoid the scouts patrolling the forest and the veil border. I'd never been as grateful for my training as I was now. I knew every inch of the forest and exactly where to cross the veil. The bond guided me, the pull to Sean becoming stronger the closer I got. The pain coursing through my body lessened with every step, too.

As soon as I crossed the veil, I called out to Sean in my mind.

Isla? You're here. I can feel you near.

I've just crossed the veil. Stay where you are. The bond is guiding me. I'll find you.

When I approached a cave, I saw Sean sitting against the stone wall, his head jerking up as I stepped inside. A smile broke out on his face as he stood and I scrambled toward him. I couldn't help it. The longing was too intense. I wrapped my arms around him.

"Mo chroi, you made it," he said, hugging me tightly.

"I told you I'd find you," I whispered, burying my head in his chest, my hands wrapped tightly around his waist. The scent of him caused my body to heat.

"I heard you in my head and felt you getting nearer. How is that possible?" Sean asked, lifting my chin so he could look into my eyes.

"It's the bond." I swallowed hard, my eyes glued to his. I saw the longing that I knew coursed through his veins, too.

"I can think of nothing but you. I want to…" He paused, licking his lips.

"I know," I said, mirroring his actions before losing control and smashing my lips against his. I couldn't help the moan that escaped as relief washed over me. All the pain vanished, replaced with something more powerful.

His lips were soft and gentle at first, then lust took over. His tongue found its way into my mouth, tasting, exploring, dancing with mine. His hands found my breasts as we sank to the ground, having no concern for the warriors tracking us. I was lost. Nothing mattered but the feeling of his hands, the taste of his lips. His hand squeezed my breast harder, his thumb flicking across my nipple. My body arched, begging for more. The slow, circular movements caused the muscles in my core to tighten. I reached for his hand, guiding it lower, coaxing him. His teeth nipped at the edge of my chin before trailing down my neck, making me gasp. His hand dipped into the waistband of my underwear. More. I needed more. I grabbed his shirt, ripping it open so I could feel his skin against mine. He shifted slightly, discarding it, then placed his lips back on mine.

He moaned into my mouth as my hands roamed his chest, stopping to tease his taut nipples.

"I want you," he whispered.

I didn't answer. I couldn't. I gripped the back of his neck and pulled him back down, my lips crushing against his. My body was on fire, the runes on my arms burning as I reached for the button of his pants.

"You sure?" he asked, gasping for breath.

"I need you now," I panted, pushing his hand between my legs, needing to feel him there.

His fingers moved slowly, caressing the nerve endings that begged for release. One finger slipped inside as another rubbed along the top of my thigh. My muscles tightened as I arched off the ground, my fingers digging into the flesh of his hips, pulling him closer. I couldn't hold out much longer.

"Please, Sean. I need you inside me now," I pleaded as I pulled at his pants, freeing him. My fingers gripped him, my thumb brushing across the tip, spreading the liquid. He felt amazing, larger than I'd imagined. My hand moved up and down the shaft as his back arched and his hips rocked. I wanted to taste him, devour every inch of his body. His fingers moved quicker, sliding in and out of me as my hand continued stroking. My lips moved to his neck, and he threw his head back. I felt my core tighten again. I was close.

My head fell back as my body arched. Sean sensed my climax approaching and placed the tip of his manhood against my entrance. I gripped his butt and pulled him home. He felt wonderful, filling me, parting me wide to accommodate his large size. He paused to let my body adjust before he started to move. Slowly at first, my climax building. My body trembled in anticipation. His hands intertwined with mine and he raised them above my head as he thrust hard, slamming into me. He pulled back and repeated the motion.

"Faster, harder," I panted as he moved inside me.

That was all it took for my body to shatter. Ecstasy took over and the world crumbled around me. Sean followed soon after, emptying his delights inside me before collapsing onto my body.

My runes burned, but instead of pain, I felt euphoria. Every nerve in my body felt alive.

Sean kissed my lips. "You're glowing," he whispered.

I peered up at him, my eyes half closed. "So are you," I said, shaking my head. He *was* glowing. I raised my arm. A soft blue light radiated from my skin. My runes were no longer black. They now formed blue patterns across my arm and down my hand. The infinity symbol now wrapped around my fingers. The mating bond was complete.

Sean's month opened wide as he looked at his arms. "Why am I blue?"

"The bond is complete," I said, watching as the glow began to fade. "We are connected for life now."

"Oh." He pulled me close once more, nuzzling the side of my face. "I'm okay with that."

I smiled up at him. For the first time in my life, I felt complete. My hands traced the muscles in his chest. He was mine.

"Again," he said, winking at me.

"Again." My lips met his.

The sound of tumbling stones outside the cave stopped

us. I placed my finger over my lips, signaling Sean to remain quiet as I got up and crept toward the entrance. More stones fell. I knew they were above us. It wouldn't take long before we were discovered.

I looked back at Sean. "Does this cave lead anywhere?"

"No. This is it," he said, spreading his arms wide.

I shrugged. We'd have to sneak out, remain hidden, and hope we weren't spotted.

A larger rock crashed to the ground outside the cave.

"They've found us," I whispered, stepping back.

Sean's solid arms wrapped around my waist. "Let them come. I won't let anything happen to you."

I knew he meant it, but I also knew he was no match for the warriors Morgan had sent. They were trained assassins, just as I was. I shook my head. "We need a diversion, a way to get out unseen."

"I'll fight," Sean said. I knew it was the bond talking. He wasn't in control of his thoughts right now.

"You can't," I whispered. "They'll kill you, and then…" I stopped. I didn't want to think about it. Now that the bond had been completed, it meant that should one of us die, the other would follow. The thought alone sent a wave of terror pulsing through my body, making the blue glow intensify. It had all but disappeared from Sean's skin, but my body started lighting up.

"What is it?" Sean asked, tensing.

"The rising," I whispered.

I'd heard stories of mated fae who obtained magical powers. They called it "the rising", an awakening of dormant energy within the body. It was rare. The last rising had been long before my time. The stories of Sheba were legendary. Her rising had been powerful…and the last time magic had been heard of in a mated couple.

I felt the energy coursing through my veins, sparks igniting at my fingertips as I shook my hands.

Sean stepped back. "This rising is what exactly?"

"It's the awakening of magic within my body," I muttered, trying to control my breathing.

A plume of dust rose from the mouth of the cave. I looked up to see Darrion standing there.

"Move out of the way, Isla," he said, taking aim at Sean.

I knew what his plan was—an arrow straight through Sean's heart. I also knew Darrion never missed.

"No," I shouted, moving closer to Sean, arms spread, blocking the shot. My body trembled and glowed bright.

Darrion flinched. "You're glowing. You completed the bond."

I nodded.

"Isla…"

The way he said my name, I heard the disgust, the bitterness.

"Shoot if you must, but be warned. I will not go down without a fight."

Darrion swallowed and stood his ground. He gripped his bow tightly, his knuckles white. "I *will* shoot you, Isla. I have no choice. You know the laws."

I watched him hesitate before pulling the string back, the arrow ready to take flight. His mouth twitched as he released the tension and the arrow flew toward us.

My hands shot out, blue light filling the space around us. The arrow bounced off it and fell to the ground.

Darrion's mouth gaped as he loosed another. The

arrow collided with the blue light and fell to the ground. I'd created a barrier that protected us. I had no idea how, but while it was there, we needed to make our escape.

I grabbed Sean's hand and pulled. "We have to go. Now."

Darrion reached out and tried to stop us, but he couldn't. The force field was impenetrable…or so I thought. Sean's fist flew through the air and struck Darrion's jaw. He stumbled before falling to the ground.

"Let's go," Sean said. We hurried past Darrion and out the entrance.

He must have been on his own because there was no sign of anyone else.

"We need to hide. They won't stop looking for us," I said, scanning our surroundings. The cave in the mountain overlooked the lake and the forest. The entrance to Faery wasn't far.

"My grandfather has a cabin about a day's journey from here. It's deep in the mountains, but we'll be safe there," Sean said, pulling me close.

It was our only option. We couldn't stay close to the veil. Not now that the bond had been completed.

The blue light around us diminished and I gripped Sean's hand tightly. "Lead the way."

We walked along the mountain trail, no sign of anyone following us.

"That was some punch. Where did you learn to fight?" I asked, turning to look at him.

He smiled before shrugging. "A man's gotta know how to protect his woman."

We moved in silence for a time, my mind replaying the

events of the day as the sun sank below the horizon. My morning had started out normal—scout the area, protect the veil, and kill any human who dares to cross. Now, after mating with a human I couldn't imagine being without, I ran from my own people, magic awakened in my veins. The rising had always seemed like a myth, a story to frighten us. I never thought it was real.

"You okay?" Sean asked, squeezing my hand.

"Yes. Just thinking about everything that's happened today."

"Me, too. I still can't wrap my head around it, though. From the moment I saw you, I haven't been able to get you out of my mind. And now, here we are, mated…as you say…and I've never been happier."

"Even though we're being hunted and they plan to kill you?"

"Even with that. If I only get one day with you, I'll meet death with a smile. You," he said, lifting my chin so he could look into my eyes, "are worth everything, even death."

I swallowed the lump in my throat, my heart thumping in my chest. His words rang true. I would gladly greet death for him.

"Let's find a place to shelter for the night. There are a lot of caves hidden in these mountains. We'll be safe."

A few minutes later, Sean found a cave and we settled in.

"What's the matter?" he asked, taking my hands in his.

"Nothing." I shook my head.

"Don't give me that. I can feel your emotions, your confusion. Talk to me."

I turned to face him. "I don't know what to do. I've lived by my orders for so long. And the rising… I always thought it was a myth."

"We'll be fine," Sean said, trying to comfort me. "We'll muddle through this together. I don't know anything about a rising, but I do know I will protect you with my life."

"Me, too," I whispered, leaning my head against his chest.

"You get some sleep. I'll take the first watch." Sean stroked my hair.

I gazed up at him, my body reacting to his touch. "I'm not tired."

His eyes bore into mine, longing and need evident.

We spent the night wrapped in each other's bodies, exploring, tasting, and owning one another.

***

The next morning, we set out for the cabin. It was a long journey, but we passed the time by chatting. We discussed everything we could think of. Occasionally, we'd glance behind us. No one followed. We were safe…for now. I knew the warriors wouldn't travel this far inland on their own. They'd scout the veil, waiting for me to return. I had no intention of ever returning, though. I'd heard what Morgan had said, the venom in her words. At least she had no idea I'd heard her, thinking the bond had forced me to leave. I snickered when I thought of the look on her face.

"What's so funny?" Sean asked, turning to me.

"I was just thinking of the look on Morgan's face when Darrion gets back."

Sean lifted his eyebrows. "That's funny, is it?"

I thought for a moment, then shook my head. "No, actually, it isn't. He'll tell her about the rising. I'd forgotten about that."

Sean giggled.

"What's funny?" I asked.

"How could you forget you glowed and created a force field?"

"I know," I said, giggling along with him. "It was amazing, right?"

"Yep." He pulled me close and kissed the top of my head.

Energy pulsed through my veins as I gazed up at him. My body longed for his touch. I saw it in his eyes, too.

I cleared my throat. "We have to keep going. How much farther?"

"Just over the next hill, but we're taking the long way so we can avoid the village."

My body shivered.

"Don't worry. You'll be safe. The cabin is secluded. It's about a mile from the village and no one ever goes out there." He squeezed my hand.

Comfort filled my body, making me smile. Sean intertwined his fingers with mine. I looked down, then gasped. "You have a rune."

A small infinity symbol circled his fingers, connecting with mine where our hands joined.

"I didn't see that earlier," he said, shaking his head.

"Me, neither. Have you more?"

Sean pulled up his sleeve. The skin of his arm was bare. "Doesn't look like it. Is this normal?"

"I don't know." There had never been a case where a fae and human bonded, so I had no idea what happened.

"Maybe I'll turn blue, as well." He grinned. I couldn't help but smile back. "Come on," he said, tugging on my hand. "Let's get you home."

I licked my lips. I liked the sound of that. Home.

It took another hour to reach the cabin. My feet ached from all the walking, so I couldn't wait to sit down.

Sean stopped when the cabin and surrounding garden came into view. The cabin was small, but it looked cozy and inviting. "Wait here," he said.

"Why? I thought you said no one came out here."

"They don't, but I want to make sure."

I looked around as he walked off. The mountain backdrop with snow-capped peaks, the small forest to the right, a trail leading down the hill to the left. I presumed it led to the village. I traced the runes on my hand and wrist, trying to figure out what all this meant. I'd resisted the bond, felt disgusted at first, but my body now yearned for Sean's. He felt like an extension of me. Life without him didn't seem possible.

I thought about our joining, his body wrapped around mine. My skin heated. I looked down and saw the blue glow appear once more. I didn't understand it. I knew it was magic coursing through my veins, but what could it do? What could *I* do?

"It's safe. Come inside."

Sean's voice pulled me from my thoughts and I moved toward the cabin.

"No one's been here," he said as I stopped beside him. "We'll be safe." He wrapped his arm around my waist and led me inside.

It was a small room with little furniture—a bed over on one side, a table by the window, and a sink beneath another window that overlooked the back of the cabin. A large, open fireplace completed the room.

"It used to be my grandfather's hunting cabin," Sean said as he watched me look around. "Few people know of its existence."

I moved around the room, my hands brushing dust off everything. It was perfect. Our own little slice of heaven.

"I'll have to go to the village for supplies, but you can rest while I'm gone. I shouldn't be more than an hour or two."

I looked up in horror. He was leaving me?

"I'll be back soon. I promise," Sean said, reaching for me. "I can't be apart from you for long."

I forced a smile, pain starting in the pit of my stomach at the thought of his absence. "Be careful," I said, cupping his cheek. "I'll die if anything happens to you."

"It won't." He placed his forehead against mine, holding my gaze before bending and capturing my lips.

My legs trembled as longing grew inside.

Sean pulled away, smirking. "I'd better go or we'll have nothing to eat later."

I watched him leave, my heart aching with every step he took.

While he was gone, I tried to rest, but it was nearly impossible. The mating bond ensured I felt his absence, and it took all my strength not to follow him.

The moment he opened the cabin door again, I ran into his arms, kissing every inch of his face. He dropped his supplies, his own kisses just as fervent, and carried me to the small bed.

"I missed you so much," he whispered against my neck.

"Me, too," I moaned as I ripped at his clothing.

An hour later, after our bodies had calmed, Sean climbed out of bed to retrieve the supplies that had spilled out onto the floor.

"I met someone in the village. Someone who said they could help."

I bolted upright. "Who? Did they follow you? It could be a trap." I grabbed my clothes and hastily dressed. "Sean?"

He turned to look at me. "They saw my rune and said they knew what it meant."

"What did you say?"

"I tried to deny it, said I didn't know what she was talking about."

"She?"

"Yeah, an old lady."

I let out a sigh of relief.

"What?" Sean asked, taking my hand in his.

"She can't be fae. We don't age like humans do. Our bodies retain the look of youth no matter what age we are."

"Good to know," he grinned, his fingers tracing the skin on my arm.

I shook my head and pulled my arm back to break the connection. I couldn't give in. Not yet. "What else did she say?" I gasped out, fighting the pull of his body.

"She said to tell you to come see her. You've been given a powerful gift and she can show you how to use it."

"I don't know, Sean. Morgan and her warriors are

looking for us. They will kill us on sight. Human and fae aren't meant to bond."

Sean took my hand and stopped me from pacing. "I know, but what if she can help? Show you how to use the blue glow?"

I laughed. "Blue glow? It's magic, Sean."

"Oh," he said, smirking. "Well, then, that's even more reason to meet her. Magic could be useful for lots of things." He pulled me closer. "Like making clothes disappear."

I swatted at his hand as his finger kneaded the soft skin above my hips. "We have to talk about this."

"We will," he whispered against my ear before trailing kisses down my neck.

I tipped my head back, his body calling to mine. "Sean…," I moaned as he lifted me, my legs wrapping around his waist.

"We'll talk later, Isla. I have to have you first."

We spent the next hour ravaging each other, yet I still wanted more. I'd heard about mated couples hiding away for weeks after the bond formed, some even longer, until they got themselves under control. The intense need to touch and satisfy one another was usually too great to ignore. Sean and I had only been mated two days.

He brushed my hair away from my face as he stroked my cheek. "What should we do about the lady in the village?"

"I don't know," I whispered. "Did she say anything else?"

"She said the rising meant great change and it hadn't been seen since Sheba."

I nodded, remembering the stories.

"She also said that without control, the magic can take over and destroy its host." He looked away.

"What else, Sean?"

He turned back to me, tears welling in his eyes. "She said we don't have a lot of time, maybe a couple weeks. The magic grows stronger each time we join. Unless you learn to harness it, use it, it will build until it explodes."

"I'll meet her, learn how to control it. I won't let anything happen to us," I said, pulling him to me. "I promise."

We held each other tightly, the fear of loss powerful. I knew it was because of the bond. Without it, I would see him as nothing but a human, one I would want to kill. I paused at that thought. Why would I want to destroy another life? Because I was told to, trained to. I'd never met a human before, yet I was willing to kill one on sight. Was I wrong? Was Morgan wrong? While I lay in bed in the Summer Court, she'd shown me a side I'd never seen before. Evil and nasty. I shuddered at the memory of her words, the venom in her voice.

"What is it, Isla?" Sean whispered.

"Sorry. Nothing. I was just thinking about my life before I met you."

"That bad, was it?"

"Not really. I trained hard and I was one of the best. I'm just wondering what it was all for."

"Let's not dwell on the past. We have our future to look forward to."

"You're right," I said, smiling up at him. "And it's going to be great. I'll learn about my magic and we'll be safe."

"Yes, we will," he said, kissing the top of my head. "Come on. Let's get some food, then we can talk some more. I want to know everything about you, mo chroi."

I frowned. "What does that mean?"

"Mo chroi means 'my heart', and that is what you are to me. My heart, my everything."

My face blushed and my heart swelled. I felt the same way, but knew it was just the mating bond, which kept me from returning the endearment. If human and fae weren't supposed to bond, my feelings were wrong, unnatural. I couldn't give in to them. Not fully.

Sean built a fire and we ate in silence, both caught in our own little world.

Sean? I questioned in my mind, testing to see if we could still communicate that way or if it had been a one-time thing.

He looked up at me, eyebrows raised. "Did you just speak in my head?"

I smirked. "I did. I wanted to see if it still worked."

Fancy little trick, isn't it? He smiled, his lips unmoving.

I laughed. "At least we can't hear each other's thoughts."

"I don't know. It might be fun. I'd love to know what you think about, Isla."

The way he said my name, so passionate, had my body heating.

I'm done eating. I think it's time for dessert, he said in my mind and winked.

"Dessert sounds good." I swallowed. "What do you have in mind?"

"How about I come over there and show you," he said, rising from his chair and stalking over to me. He reached for my hand and pulled me up flush against his hard body. "I'd like *you* for dessert, Isla."

I swallowed the lump in my throat, my heart racing as his hands traced the curve of my hips and squeezed my bum. A soft moan escaped as I wrapped my arms around his neck and pulled his face to mine. "I like the sound of dessert," I whispered, then crushed my lips to his.

CHAPTER FOUR

I slept soundly that night, safe in the comfort of Sean's arms. All thoughts of Morgan, the rising, and my imminent death vanished. Sean and I dressed and prepared for the day ahead.

"Are you ready?" he asked, slipping his arms around my waist.

"As ready as I'll ever be," I said, shrugging.

He hugged me tightly. "It'll be fine. You'll see. We're not committing to anything. We're just going to listen to what she has to say."

I nodded. I wasn't sure I was ready for all this. What if it were a trap, a way to capture us? "You sure it's safe?" I asked.

"She's human, if that's what you're asking."

"Okay. Let's go before I change my mind."

The walk to the village was pleasant, but I couldn't shake the panic that crept through my body. Each step took us closer to the inevitable. What if I couldn't control the magic? What if they took Sean? My palms were sweaty, my steps wavering.

Sean took my hand in his and squeezed it gently. "Stop worrying, Isla."

"I'm trying not to," I whispered, "but I can't help it."

He grinned. "Think of all the fun we can have when you figure out this whole magic thing."

I smiled. It definitely would be fun.

***

The village was quiet. Then again, it was early in the morning.

"How do we find her?" I asked, looking down the long street, houses on either side.

"She said to go to the end of the street, turn right, then follow the road out of the village. She lives about a half-mile out in a yellow cottage with a stone wall, roses covering the front."

The fact we didn't have to stay in the village calmed my nerves somewhat, but the closer we came to the yellow cottage, the more panic took over.

"What if it's a trap, Sean?"

"It's not," he said, trying to reassure me. "Besides, you can shield us. We'll be fine."

"But what if—"

Sean placed his finger against my lips. "Stop worrying, Isla. I won't let anything happen to you. I promise." He bent down and placed a soft kiss on my forehead. "Come on. We're almost there."

My hands trembled at the sight of the cottage, but I took a deep breath as we walked through the gates. Roses in full bloom covered the front, their sweet scent filling my nose.

"Beautiful, aren't they?" Sean asked, smiling at me. "Almost as beautiful as you."

"They are," I said, taking in all the colors. White roses were mixed with deep reds, while pinks and oranges were interwoven around the windows. This took a lot of planning and care. I instantly knew I'd like this woman.

Sean knocked on the door. I held my breath, having no idea what to expect as it creaked open. A white-haired lady with deep wrinkles on her face stood looking at us. She seemed so old, except for her eyes. They sparkled, a crisp, clear green that had me frowning. They didn't match the rest of her aged body.

"I've been expecting you," she said, looking from Sean to me. "I actually thought you'd be here yesterday. Not to worry. Come in. There's much to discuss."

I glanced at Sean. He squeezed my hand as we followed her into a small living room. There were two couches facing each other, a large open fireplace, and a bookcase filled with old books. It was warm and cozy, and the fresh smell of roses filled the air.

"Sit yourselves down. I won't bite," she said, waving at the couch. "Can I get you some tea?"

"Please," Sean answered as we took a seat on the faded green couch. It was worn, but comfortable.

I relaxed a little. "You sure it's safe?" I asked Sean once more.

"Perfectly. If you want to leave at any time, just tell me. We have that mind thing, don't we?"

We do, I said in my mind and grinned at him.

I wonder how it works. Do you hear my thoughts, Isla?

No. I only hear when you are speaking directly to me.
Maybe we should ask her.
No.

He frowned. *Why not?*
We need to keep some secrets to ourselves.

"Don't mind me," the old lady said, coming back into the room. "I see you've managed the mindcom then?"

"The what?" Sean asked.

"Mindcom. Well, that's what I like to call it anyway. How long have you had it?"

"Since the runes first appeared," I answered.

The old lady set the tray she'd been carrying on the small table between the couches. "My name's May."

"I'm Sean, and this is Isla."

"There's lots to talk about, but let's have tea first," she said, pouring three cups.

"So, how long since the bond?" She looked at me.

"A couple days." I reached for the cup.

"It's strong then," she muttered, sitting on the opposite couch. "Are you royalty?"

I gasped. "No. I'm a warrior in the Summer Court."

"Ah, one of Morgan's." She nodded.

"How do you know of Morgan?"

"I know a lot, girl." I could have sworn I saw her eyes flash.

"You know about the rising, the magic?"

"Oh yes, child. I know all about it and the danger you're in if you don't learn to harness and control it."

She picked up her cup and brought it to her lips, blowing gently before taking a sip. "The magic is like energy. It builds inside you, growing stronger and stronger.

Kinda like a pot boiling. If the lid isn't lifted and the steam allowed to escape... Well, you know what happens."

My mouth hung open. I didn't like the thought of something building and growing inside me. "How do I stop that from happening?"

"You learn to use it."

"That simple, eh?" Sean asked, placing his cup back on the table.

"I never said it was simple, young man. Far from it. But with practice and training, it's a powerful force and can do a world of good."

"How do you know all this?" I asked, returning my cup to the table. I hadn't acquired a taste for this hot drink called tea. It tasted bitter in my mouth.

May looked at us, deep in thought. Finally, she let out a sigh. "How old do you think I am?"

"Seventy, maybe eighty," Sean said.

"And you?" May asked, looking at me.

"I don't know," I answered truthfully. "Your body is aged, but your eyes shine as brightly as a youngling."

"Clever girl," she said, smirking. "I am nearly 1,000 years old. I witnessed the first rising, the freedom that Sheba brought, and the destruction that followed when Mallory betrayed her. I was one of her closest companions, so my punishment was this. The body of a human, aged and decrepit, but the mind, knowledge, and lifespan of a fae.

I gasped. "Who would do such a thing?"

"Morgan's father, along with the other court kings. It was a long time ago now, but I've been waiting. Sheba promised the rising would come again, that freedom would be granted once more. I'd stopped believing it...until I met

Sean yesterday and saw the rune on his fingers. I knew then the time had come. Finally, someone to release me from my prison."

"I don't understand. How can fae become human?"

May lowered her head and took a deep breath. "What you see before you, Isla, is what will happen to you if Sean dies. My mate was killed, but before they could get to me, I escaped. Call it luck or fate, whatever you like, but I am the lone survivor of that time. I've called it a curse for a long time, but seeing you both…" She stopped and raised her gaze to meet mine. "You can create change, bring unity to the lands once more."

I shook my head. "I'm not sure I can. I know nothing of this world you speak of. I've only heard stories and whispers. Morgan searches for me as we speak. All I want is to know how to protect us and prevent the magic from overpowering me. Sean told me what you said yesterday."

"I see a lot of Sheba in you, child. You are stronger than you think."

"I'm not sure I want to be." My hands fumbled in my lap. "I just want to be safe."

"I will teach you all I know. The magic is powerful, but to use it, you need to feel. You need to let your emotions feed it, nurture it. That is how it works."

I thought about what May said. It made sense. The force field I'd created had come out of fear. A protection for Sean and me. The blue glow igniting my skin came from love, happiness. I looked at her, questions flooding my mind. "How long will it take?"

"That depends on you, Isla. I can only depart my knowledge. It is you who must access your emotions and work with them. Certain magic requires certain emotions. You must be able to tap into them at will."

I listened, nodding. Sean remained quiet, reaching for my hand and squeezing it tightly.

"What are you thinking, child?" May asked, watching me closely.

I cleared my throat. "The emotions, the magic… Do I have to sustain them for the magic to last?"

"Not always. There are spells that can be created to last a lifetime, others that hold until the emotion passes."

It was so much information to take in. My head throbbed, but there was one final question I had to ask. "What happens to Sean if they kill me?"

May sighed. "He will feel as if his heart has been ripped from his body. Grief will consume him, and his body will cease to function."

"So, he'll die," I blurted out.

"Yes, Isla. Should you lose your life, he will die. That is how the mating bond works. Two souls united, living in unison, tied together for eternity. Should one die, the other will perish."

"But *you* didn't die."

"No. I received a fate much worse. I feel the loss of my mate every single day. I feel him trapped somewhere, calling to me, but I can never reach him."

"But he died. You said—"

"I know what I said, child." May stood. "I watched as they plunged the knife through his heart. Felt the pain of it ripping through my own. I fled."

The confusion on my face made her continue.

"I was hiding, on my way to rescue him from the

dungeons. I didn't see the sorcerer until it was too late. They knew I'd feel his pain and try to rescue him, which was their plan. I watched him take his last breath. Whatever spell they used kept his essence alive, and me with it, but without contact, without seeing him, this is what I've become. Our bond believes him to be alive, so that is the only reason I still breathe."

I didn't know what to say. It didn't make sense. Her mate was killed. She should have died.

"The bond between fae and human is different. The normal rules don't apply, Isla. I cannot be certain what would happen to Sean or to you."

Sean stood. "I think that's enough for today. You look tired, May. We should let you rest."

"I haven't felt this alive in eons, but you're right. You and Isla need time to discuss things. I will be here when you decide," May said, sitting down once more.

"But I want to train, to learn. I will not let Morgan win!" I shouted, causing them both to turn in my direction. "If I hold this magic, I want to know how to use it. She's coming for me, and I plan to be ready. Will you teach me, May?"

"Are you sure, mo chroi?" Sean asked.

"Yes." I moved to where he stood. "I won't let anything tear us apart. I will fight to my last breath."

He smiled and wrapped his arms around me, kissing me on the forehead.

"When do we begin?" I asked May.

She smiled. "Tomorrow. Be here early."

***

May was an excellent teacher. She showed me how to tap into the magic, pull it from the inner recesses of my body, and set it free.

"Control," she said, "is the key to mastery, Isla."

I hadn't understood its meaning at the time, but as the weeks passed, it became clear that having access to magic was useless without understanding how to use it. I could wield it and send it out in blasts. I could shield myself, too, but I still couldn't control the outcome.

"What am I doing wrong?" I shouted in frustration after the third week.

"You're focused on anger, using it as your predominant emotion," May said, jumping out of the way as a blast of blue light shot from my fingers.

"But I *am* angry. I don't want anything to happen to Sean or me."

May moved toward me. "Control comes from mastering your emotions, Isla. You need to feel what you want the magic to do. Caress it. Let it become a part of you, a part you love. The power of love is the greatest of all."

My shoulders fell. "You want me to think loving thoughts? Impossible. I cannot feel love for Morgan or the warriors she sends after me."

She sighed. "You're not listening, Isla. I don't want you to think loving thoughts for those vermin. I want you to love the magic. Let's try something."

May stood in front of me. "I want you to summon your magic. Let it build, then let it loose upon me."

I stepped back. "Are you mad? It will destroy you."

May shook her head. "You must control it, Isla. Tell it

what to do. I want you to close your eyes and think of Sean, think of the love you feel for him. Visualize the magic caressing his body. Can you do that?"

I looked at her, eyes wide. "I think so."

"Good. Begin."

I did as May instructed, letting the magic build, feeling its destructive power.

"Think of Sean," May whispered.

I concentrated, visualizing Sean in front of me. I tried blocking out the anger and fear, focusing only on our connection, our love.

"Good. Very good," May said. I heard her chuckle. "Open your eyes, Isla."

I did and gasped. Blue tendrils of energy circled May, stroking her softly. She was alive, unharmed.

"You did it." She had a big grin on her face. "Now, you are ready."

"Ready?"

"Yes. I could not teach you anything until you learned control."

I shook my hands, the magic disappearing. "What have we been doing these past three weeks then?"

"Practicing," May said, turning toward the cottage. "Now the learning will begin."

I followed her.

"Sit. I'll make tea," she said, disappearing into the kitchen.

I obeyed, but I was on edge. What did she mean by learning? I thought that was what I'd been doing.

May returned minutes later with two cups of tea. I was getting used to the bitter taste now. I took a sip and looked up at her. "What did you mean by learning?"

"Spells," she muttered, bringing the cup to her lips and blowing on the hot liquid. "It's time to add spells to the magic, Isla."

"Oh."

"You'll see," she smiled. "Now, drink up. There's lots more to do today."

After finishing my tea, I followed May through the house. When she pushed open a door, my breath caught. I didn't know she had a library. Row upon row of books filled the floor-to-ceiling shelves.

"What is this?" I gasped.

"The learning," May replied, stepping into the room. She must have seen the horrified look on my face. "We'll start easy. Don't worry, Isla. You'll be fine."

I wasn't so sure, but I nodded and followed. My eyes took in the room. Two chairs sat on either side of a fireplace with a small table in between.

"We'll be here for a while, so you may as well sit," May said, running her hands along a row of books. "Ah, there you are."

"Are all these books about magic?" I asked.

"Good Lord, no," May gasped. "I have to keep up appearances, you know. Most of these are just stories, literary classics. Innocent-looking to the human eye. It takes a magical touch to read what's really inside the ones that hold spells."

I frowned. This was all getting a little too confusing.

"Here. Let me show you," May said, handing me the book she'd chosen.

I took it and read the title—*A Tale of Two Cities*.

"A classic," she grinned. "Now, place your hand on the cover and tap in to your magic. Then repeat the words I tell you."

I nodded and felt inside for the now familiar stirring.

"Eludious Incantus," May said, and I repeated.

When the book shook in my hands, I dropped it. I leaned down to pick it up, seeing the cover had changed. I now held a black, leather-bound tome that looked older than time itself. I turned it over in my hands and looked at May for permission to open it.

"Go ahead," she said, nodding.

I lifted the leather binding and read the inscription inside the cover.

May, my dearest companion.
Inside these pages is the power to continue what I have begun.
Keep it safe until the one with my power surfaces.
She will know what to do.
Sheba

I raised my eyes to May. "You think *I'm* the one?"

"I know you are, child. Only the one can reveal the words."

"But you know what it said."

"I read that inscription before Sheba fell." May lowered her gaze. This had to be hard for her, too.

"I'm sorry. I didn't mean to be insensitive. I just… I don't know what to make of all this."

"You don't need to do anything yet, Isla. All you must do is learn. You can decide then."

I nodded and began to turn the pages.

***

I spent the next two weeks learning to use the spells, along with my magic. They enhanced it, gave it purpose, gave me purpose. I could wield my magic into different shapes and forms, create storms, and harness the power of nature at will.

"You're doing great," May said, smiling at me as I conjured an illusion of myself.

"I don't see the point of this spell," I muttered, watching a mirror image of myself walk around in circles.

"If there's a battle, it will help distract the enemy. They won't know it's not you."

"I suppose," I shrugged. I wasn't in the mood today. I felt off. I couldn't put my finger on it, but something in me felt different.

"Want to try something else?" May asked, flipping the pages of the book.

"Anything in there to conjure food? I'm starving," I said, cutting off the flow of magic. My double disappeared.

May laughed. "Come on. Let's take a break. I could do with some lunch, too."

I followed her inside. Over lunch, we talked about the different spells I'd learned. Most of them were battle strategies—turning my magic into deadly arrows, using the wind to my advantage, and of course, cloning myself.

"What is it?" May asked. "You've been frowning for the past ten minutes, Isla."

"I'm not sure." I shrugged. "Something's off. I just don't know what."

"You worried about something?"

I thought about it for a moment. "It's been too quiet. Why haven't they come after me yet?"

May sighed. "If I had to guess, I'd say Morgan is planning. That one is wicked, but don't worry, Isla. You'll be ready."

I nodded. She was right. Strategy was something Morgan excelled at. "I need to learn to shield Sean."

"But you can already."

"When I'm with him, yes, but I need to be able to protect him when I'm not. Morgan will be watching, waiting for him to be on his own. That's when she'll strike. I just know it."

"You could shield the cabin, maybe the garden. I'm not sure how far the shield can extend, though."

"I'd like to try."

"How about tomorrow?" May said, bringing her cup to her lips. "I'll see what I can find in my books."

"You have more books on magic?" I gasped. "You didn't mention them."

"Magic is a dangerous thing, Isla. It's not so much about the power. It's about how you use it. The intention must always be positive. Always."

That couldn't be right. May was teaching me spells of destruction, spells that could harm. How was that positive?

"Your intention behind the spell is positive," May said, obviously reading my expression. "The spells you've learned may cause harm, but the dominant intention behind them is protection. There is a difference."

"I don't get it. I could very well kill someone with my arrows. Isn't that negative?"

"Not necessarily," May sighed. "When you cast your spells, what are you thinking?"

I stared at her. She was right. Every spell I'd used so far had been with the intention of protecting myself, protecting Sean.

"Now you get it," May said, clasping her hands.

"What happens if the intention isn't positive?" I asked.

"The magic becomes dark, twisted, evil. You lose yourself to the power."

"Have you seen it happen?"

"No, I haven't," she sighed. "Let's stop for today and begin again in the morning. We'll work on building a shield."

"Okay."

CHAPTER FIVE

My head was fuzzy, my stomach churning. "I don't feel right," I said as Sean placed a cup of tea beside me.

"You need rest. You and May have been at it non-stop for weeks. It's your body telling you to slow down, Isla."

"I can't. Do you think Morgan's slowing down? She's not. She's out there plotting and planning. I need to be ready."

"There's only so much you can do, mo chroi. Taking a day to rest will make all the difference."

"I can't, Sean. Our lives depend on it. Don't you see that?"

He reached for my hand. "All I see is you running yourself ragged, Isla. I see you tired and cranky, and…" He lowered his gaze and ran his fingers through his hair. "I'm worried about you."

I squeezed his hand. He lifted his eyes to mine. "I'm doing this for us. Morgan won't stop. She is coming. I know it."

"Fine," Sean said, letting go of my hand. "But I'm coming with you today. If you don't feel any better, we're coming home again."

"Fine," I huffed as I picked up my tea. I took a sip, my stomach rolling. "Is the milk off?"

"No, why?"

"My tea tastes funny." I pushed it away.

***

May was waiting by the back porch and looked up when she saw us coming. "What's wrong?"

"Isla's not feeling well," Sean answered before I had the chance to speak.

May walked toward me and took my hand. "Are you okay?"

"I'm fine," I snapped, pulling my hand free. "Sean's over exaggerating. My stomach's a little off, that's all."

May nodded. "Let's get to work then."

We spent all day working on my shield. By the end, I managed to extend it ten meters, but I was exhausted.

"It takes time," May said, patting my arm.

"How long?"

"I've no idea. As long as it takes. Go home and get some rest. We'll practice again tomorrow. I'll come to you. It's time we focused on the cabin."

***

The next morning, I woke with severe nausea and a thumping headache.

"You okay?" Sean asked as I stumbled to the table.

"Just a little dizzy," I said, plonking down into the chair.

"You're doing too much, Isla."

"Maybe," I mumbled.

An hour later, the dizziness and nausea had passed. When May arrived, she took one look at me and shook her head. "Feeling sick again today?"

"I'm okay now. Let's get started."

By the end of the day, I'd managed to shield Sean, myself, May, and about two meters of ground.

"That's good," May said. "You were able to shield all three of us. That's really good."

I wasn't as impressed. I had a terrible feeling in the pit of my stomach that time was running out. I had to learn to make the shield bigger…and soon.

***

For the next week, the nausea came every morning, staying a little longer each day. I attributed it to all the practice draining my body. By the second week, vomiting accompanied the nausea and I was forced to stay in bed.

"I have to get up, Sean. May will be here shortly."

"You are staying in bed," he said, arms folded across his chest. "There's something not right here."

"I have to practice. We don't know when Morgan will find us, and I'm not ready yet."

"Just stay in bed until May gets here. We'll see what she has to say. Please, Isla."

"Fine," I said, lying back down. I was relieved, even if I didn't show it. I felt dreadful.

Sean met May at the door and led her into the cabin.

"Isla, what's the matter?" she asked, making her way over to the bed.

"I think all the training is draining me. I just can't seem to function this morning."

May raised an eyebrow. "What are your symptoms?"

I explained about the nausea and the vomiting and how it passed as the day wore on.

"It can't be. You can't," May whispered.

"Can't be what?" I said, sitting up straight.

"It's not possible," she continued, pacing back and forth beside my bed.

"May, spit it out. What's wrong with me?"

She stopped and turned to face me, her face pale. "I… I think you could be with child."

My mouth fell open. Words sat on the tip of my tongue, but I couldn't get them out.

"We're going to have a baby?" Sean asked, a slight lilt in his voice. "That's wonderful news, isn't it?"

May and I looked at each other.

"It *is* good news, isn't it?" Sean repeated, looking from May to me.

I shook my head. "I don't know."

We both looked at May. She hadn't said a word.

"May?"

"It's never happened before, Isla. I didn't even know it was possible. This changes everything. If word gets out…"

I realized the seriousness of her words, a cold shiver spreading across my body. "Are you sure? It might be in one of your books."

"I'm sure," May said, moving toward the bed again.

"Fae and humans have never bred. I don't know what this means, Isla." Her tone was grave.

"Maybe I'm not with child. Maybe it is the magic." I didn't really believe it, but it felt like the right thing to say.

"We'll know soon enough," May said, taking my hand in hers. "Soon, you won't be able to hide it."

"Tea?" Sean asked, trying to ease the tension.

We both nodded and sat at the table, deep in our own thoughts.

A baby. I couldn't believe it. What would it be like? So many questions swirled in my mind as I automatically placed my hand on my stomach. There were three of us to protect now.

***

May was right. Within weeks, my stomach rounded and began to grow. The daily practice took on a whole new meaning. I wasn't just protecting my mate. I was now protecting our child, which seemed to increase my strength.

By the time I was close to six months pregnant, I'd managed to shield the entire cabin and the small garden in front.

Although May searched through every book she could find, there was no mention of a fae and human baby anywhere.

Sean was thrilled and couldn't wait to meet our little one. He spent every evening talking to my stomach, stroking it gently, and giggling every time the baby kicked. That was on top of trying to stop me from doing anything.

"Boy or girl?" he asked one evening as we snuggled in

front of the fire.

I smiled up at him. "I don't mind. You?"

"Oh, I want a little girl. Another you who I can spoil rotten."

I laughed. "And have you a name chosen for this little girl?"

"A few." He winked. "But I'd like to hear your suggestions."

I hadn't really given it much thought. I'd been so focused on protecting us and building the shield that names hadn't entered my mind. I looked up at him. "I don't know. What did you come up with?"

Sean smiled. "I was thinking Aisling. It means 'dreams' in Irish. Our dream baby."

"I like that," I said, sounding the name out.

"She'll make our dreams come true, won't you, Aisling?" Sean said, grinning, touching my stomach.

"I hope it's a girl. I'd hate for you to be disappointed, Sean."

"I won't be disappointed," he replied.

***

"I'd like to try something different today," May said the next morning.

"Okay," I replied around a mouthful of bread. My appetite seemed insatiable.

"I'm not sure if it can be done, but I was thinking—"

"What?" I cut her off. My mood was sour. I felt heavy and cumbersome and wasn't in the mood to listen to anyone.

May scowled at me. "Just because you're pregnant doesn't mean I'll put up with your nonsense, Isla."

"Sorry," I mumbled.

"As I was saying, I want to try something different. You can shield the cabin and the garden, but I'm wondering if you can shield two things at once."

My head snapped up. May smiled, knowing she had my full attention. "Sean has to go to the village for supplies every week, and you're getting too big to go with him. I think it's time to try two shields."

I nodded. "I'm ready."

"Sean?" May called.

He came rushing in. "Is it time? Is the baby coming?"

"No." I smiled at him. "Not yet. May wants to try something and we need you for it."

"Okay," he said, wiping his hands on his trousers. "Where do you want me?"

We walked outside. Well, they walked. I waddled.

"Shield everything first," May said.

I followed her instructions.

"Sean, I want you to step outside the shield. Isla, try and shield Sean and the cabin at the same time. You're going to be casting two separate shields and holding both."

"I'll try," I said, sitting down on the porch seat. I pulled on the magic and focused my attention on Sean. The shield automatically grew around him, but disappeared from the cabin.

"Hold the shield," May said. "Let's see how far Sean can go."

I nodded. May instructed him to walk toward the village. "When the shield evaporates, turn back."

Sean left. I felt the shield protecting him. "What if I can't do both?" I asked, turning to May.

"We've still got time to practice," she said, patting my knee.

"Have there been any fae sightings?"

"A few, but they haven't reached the village yet. You're still safe, Isla."

An hour later, Sean arrived back, the shield still surrounding him.

"I made it all the way to the village. I didn't bother seeing how far I could go after that."

"Excellent," May said. "Isla, do you think you can try for two shields again?"

"I can try," I said, sitting up a little straighter.

"I want you to feel the shield around Sean, focus on reinforcing it first, then set the intention to create a second one. See two of them in your mind. One around the cabin, one around Sean."

I closed my eyes and followed May's instructions. I felt the magic pull in two directions. May squeezed my knee.

"It's working," she whispered.

I opened my eyes. Sean was cocooned inside a blue orb, and from where I sat, I saw the boundary of another shield just off the porch.

"You did it, Isla," Sean said, coming closer to the cabin.

May smiled. "Well done. You can let it go now. You probably need to rest."

***

I spent the next month reinforcing both shields until it took little effort to create and hold them.

"I think you're almost ready," May said, squeezing my hand.

"In more ways than one." I rubbed my stomach.

May smiled. "I'll be back tomorrow. You get some rest."

I sat on the porch, watching her leave. This stranger had become like a mother to me.

"You look happy," Sean said, taking the seat beside me.

"I am. I don't think I've ever been happier."

"Me, too." He leaned over and kissed my forehead. "Come on. I'll help you inside."

"You saying I can't get up?" I teased.

"Would I do that?" He took my hands and helped me up. He was right, though. I found it more difficult to move every day.

We sat and cuddled on the couch for the evening, both lost in our own little worlds.

"Do you want some tea?" Sean asked, breaking the silence.

"I'm okay." I smiled at him.

I still couldn't believe he was mine and we were about to bring a new life into the world. The moment I felt my baby moving inside me, all the anxiety left, replaced with wonder and excitement.

"You tired?" Sean asked, brushing a stray piece of hair behind my ear.

"Always," I mumbled, leaning into his touch.

"Let's get you to bed then."

***

I woke early, the sun barely above the horizon. The baby kicked and wriggled. I smiled as I maneuvered myself out of bed. I wasn't normally up first, so I thought I'd treat Sean to breakfast and actually be ready when May arrived.

"This is a treat," Sean said around a mouthful of porridge an hour later.

"I was awake early."

"Our little one messing with her mom again?" he asked, grinning.

"She's lively this morning," I said, rubbing my stomach. "I'm going to sit out on the porch and wait for May."

"Okay, mo chroi."

The sun was warm on my face as I watched for May. It didn't take long for her to arrive, waving from the tree line as she stepped into view.

She hadn't walked a hundred meters before the fae pounced. They caught me by surprise, making me scream. May fell to the ground. Sean raced from the house as I raised my hand. Blue light shot forth, knocking the attackers to the ground.

"Shield, Isla," Sean screamed, taking in the scene

I froze as Morgan stepped from the tree line, twenty fae with her.

"Shield, Isla!" Sean shouted, pulling on my arm.

I blinked and finally registered him beside me.

"Shield," he said, pointing at the fae getting closer.

I raised my hands and instantly sealed us inside a blue bubble. "May…," I whispered.

Sean gripped my hand.

Morgan moved closer. "What have you done?" she

screamed. "You are an abomination, Isla. You will die for this." She turned to the fae guards. "Break the shield…now. Kill the human and bring her to me."

Sean gripped my hand tighter. I felt him tremble beside me as arrows flew toward us. Each strike bounced off the shield, and I took a deep breath.

Morgan's screams grew louder, more terrifying. The baby kicked. "Go inside, Sean. I've got this," I whispered, feeling my magic grow.

"I'm not leaving you. We stand together."

"Please."

"Isla, I'm inside the shield. I'm not leaving you."

"Fine," I said. "Help me up."

I struggled to my feet, my hand resting protectively over my stomach.

The fae stopped, hands flying to their mouths as they gasped. "What is she?" I heard one of them say.

My eyes met Morgan's. She looked horrified. "What have you done?!" she screamed. "Fae and human can't mix."

I smirked as I gripped Sean's hand. Time to end this.

"Kill them both," Morgan screamed.

I watched as more arrows flew toward us. The shield rippled. In my panic, I threw my magic out, watching as, one by one, the fae crumpled to the ground. Morgan stood there, mouth gaping.

"You will leave now," I screamed, "or face the same fate. You will *not* come back here."

Her icy glare pinned me to the spot. "This is not over," she spat. "You will pay for what you've done, Isla."

I felt my resolve slipping, the shield faltering. My legs

wobbled, so I leaned into Sean for support. I couldn't let Morgan see my energy wane. "Leave here now, Morgan," I shouted, sending bolts of blue light into the ground beside her. "I will kill you if you come any closer."

She lifted her gaze to mine. "I'll be back, Isla, and magic won't protect you."

With that, she turned and left.

I flopped back onto the bench and sobbed. "May."

"Shield me," Sean said. "I'll go and get her."

I nodded.

After Sean retrieved May's body, we buried her and said our goodbyes.

***

I didn't sleep for two days.

"You have to sleep, Isla," Sean pleaded.

"I can't. She'll be back. I must be ready. I should have killed her."

"No. That's not you, mo chroi."

I gave him a small smile. He was right, as usual. I wasn't a killer.

"You need rest. Think of the baby. Please, Isla."

"I am!" I shouted, instantly regretting it. "I'm sorry. I don't…" I swallowed. "I don't know what to do."

"It's okay, love. We'll do this together. Your shield will hold, keeping us safe while you sleep."

I nodded as he wrapped his arms around me and pulled me in close, my eyes closing.

***

There was no sign of Morgan or any fae the following day or the day after that. I kept the shield up around the cabin at all times. It gave me a small sense of comfort. Sean had buried May in the garden inside the shield barrier, which was where I now found myself. I sobbed over the mound of dirt.

"I'm so sorry I wasn't quick enough, May. I didn't see them."

I placed my hand on the ground. I couldn't do this without her. I didn't know how. I sat there and wept, my body shattered.

"There you are," Sean said, placing a hand on my shoulder.

I looked up at him, my tear-stained face revealing the depth of my grief.

"Isla," Sean said, kneeling beside me and hugging me tightly. "May wouldn't want you to grieve like this."

"I can't help it," I sobbed. "I feel lost without her."

"I know, baby. I know." He stroked my hair. "Come on. Let's get you inside. It looks like a storm is on the way."

I let him help me to my feet and guide me back indoors.

"You need to rest," he said, placing a blanket around me as I sat by the fire. His hand settled on my round stomach. "This little one will be here soon."

I forced a smile and nodded. I was tired. More tired than I'd ever been.

When Sean brought me a cup of tea, he stood there, shifting from foot to foot.

"What's wrong?" I asked.

"I have to go into the village for supplies before the storm hits." My eyes shot to his. "I'll be okay, Isla. You can shield me. I'll be back before you know it."

"I don't want you to go. What if…" I didn't finish. I couldn't.

Sean knelt beside me. "I'll be fine, mo chroi. You won't even notice I'm gone."

I gripped his hand. I didn't want to let go.

"I promise," he said, pressing his lips to mine. "Nothing will keep me away from you. Both of you."

I took in a deep breath. May believed in me. Sean believed in me. I could do this. I'd already beaten Morgan back, saw the fear in her eyes as I eradicated her men. She won't be back anytime soon. She was no match for magic.

Finding my resolve, I placed my hands on Sean's cheeks and looked deep into his eyes. "I'll be waiting for you. Always."

CHAPTER SIX

The candle burned, making shadows dance around the small cabin. The wind had picked up and battered against the window. I sat watching, waiting, and praying all would be well. I knew Sean was protected by my shield, but an uneasy feeling crept in, causing my mind to wander. My magic shielded him from Morgan, but I knew the depths she'd go to seek her so-called justice. For five years, she'd trained me to become one of her assassins, but now she viewed me as the enemy, the evil entity I'd once hunted. A shiver crept up my spine as I thought of the dangers Sean and I would face, the lengths I'd gone through to protect us and our unborn child. Maybe I should have destroyed her that day.

May had proclaimed that a time of great change drew close and our hiding would soon end. The love we shared would prove that change was possible. We no longer needed to live in fear of humans discovering our existence. I would make sure all Faery knew this, no matter the cost. I would do it for May.

I brushed away the tears that threatened to spill as I thought of her and all she'd taught me, her body falling at the hands of those she once called her own. I felt my magic build inside, anger and grief fueling it. Remembering May's warning, I forced the emotions down. No good would come of them. Not right now.

The storm outside raged on. Misshapen lightning lit the sky, the loud claps of thunder sounding forced. Nature seemed out of balance. I felt it in my core as I sat and watched destruction rain down upon the mountain. Sean would return soon. My hand caressed my swollen stomach, soothing my heart as I thought of him.

You'll be here soon, little one.

The flame flickered. I tensed, sensing Morgan. She was here, but not here. I could smell her presence, yet the cabin remained empty. I pulled on my magic, ready for whatever was to happen. My shield was intact, as was the one surrounding Sean.

Sean, can you hear me? I asked through our bond. He didn't reply. *Sean?*

The baby kicked, the shadows creeping closer.

A sharp pain ripped through my stomach. I bent over the small table. My baby couldn't come yet. Sean wasn't here. *Sean,* I shouted in my mind once more. *You need to hurry. I think the baby's coming.*

No reply.

"You'll be here soon, little one. We can't wait to meet you," I whispered.

Upon hearing my voice, I felt her move inside. She was strong, her energy unlike anything I'd ever felt before. So pure, so good. I couldn't wait to hold her, teach her of this world. I wondered about the power she would hold and if my fae gifts would transfer to her. It didn't matter either way. Sean and I had defied the odds and created this new life. Stroking my stomach relieved the panic somewhat, and I took a deep breath in.

A cold breeze brushed across my face and I froze. "Morgan," I gasped. She was here, watching me. She was in the cabin, but how? My shield was up. She couldn't get through it.

A sharp pain shot through my stomach again, making me groan. I rubbed small circles over it to try and ease the agony.

"Not yet, little one. Not yet."

It was useless. Another sharp pain and my water broke. My baby was coming. I stood from the table in front of the window and struggled to the small bed in the corner of the cabin. The pain intensified, the contractions coming too quickly, too soon. I pulled back the blankets and waited for the pain to subside before maneuvering myself onto the cold sheets.

Sean, I shouted in my head once more. *She's coming. Hurry.*

I thought I heard Morgan laugh. My eyes scanned every inch of the cabin, but it remained empty. It must be the labor, my mind imagining the worst.

As I took in deep breaths to ease the pain, I thought of the bets Sean and I had made on who our daughter would look like. Sean's prediction was she'd have dark curls and deep green eyes.

"Just like your mother," he'd murmured to my

stomach.

I laughed. "What if she looks like you? She could have soft blonde hair and blue eyes like yours, and pointed ears like mine."

We'd spent hours guessing about our unborn child and the life she would lead. Sean wanted to teach her to fish and hunt. I planned to teach her of her fae heritage and all the lies and wrongdoings that had been done. I wanted her to know the truth and make up her own mind, create her own destiny.

Another sharp pain had me gripping the sheets and struggling not to scream. "Where are you?" I called out. Sean should have been back. He'd been gone for over two hours. It didn't take that long to go to the village and back. I felt for the shield that surrounded him. It was still intact.

Shadows moved at the foot of my bed. I watched in horror as they formed into shapes.

"You're too late," I shouted. "You can't stop it now."

Morgan, along with the queens of the Autumn and Winter Courts, materialized, dressed in long, flowing gowns, hair immaculate. Their eyes glowed as they scowled. They moved closer to each other, whispering, hovering at the foot of my bed. I couldn't hear what they said, nor did I care. I had more important things to contend with, like the intense pain ripping through my stomach.

"Come on, Sean. Where are you?" I whispered as the tears streamed down my face.

"He won't be coming," they spoke in unison.

My head snapped up. "If you've hurt him, I swear—"

"We've sealed the area. A force field, a bit like your shield, has hidden the cabin from him. We've also silenced your mindchat. He won't be able to find his way back or hear you call out to him." They laughed.

I felt my magic surging, anger roaring through my veins.

"He's probably walking around in circles or banging into the force field as we speak," Mayze, the queen of the Autumn Court, said, making the others laugh again.

I glared at them, sparks of energy flying from my fingertips.

"Save your energy," Morgan spoke. "You will need it."

I didn't know what she meant, but her words sent a chill through my bones. Her eyes were black and cruel as she sneered at my body. I reached for the glass of water on the bedside table and gulped it down. Sweat beaded on my forehead as I fought to control my breathing, calm my body. If I could just stop the contractions, I could deal with Morgan and the queens, lift the veil they'd placed around me.

I rubbed my stomach in small, soothing circles. *Just wait a little longer. Please.*

When the pain subsided, I regained control. Bringing my gaze up to meet theirs, I smiled. It wasn't a friendly smile, but one of pure hatred. "*Get out!*" I screamed, raising my hands and pulling at the magic that flowed through my veins. I felt it moving, rippling to the surface, as light began to dance across my skin.

"You can't stop us, Isla. You don't have the power or the strength."

"Do I not?" I spat, sending a bolt of lightning toward them.

Morgan jumped back, but Mayze froze. The magic

caught her gown, igniting it. I laughed as she flapped her arms and danced around the foot of my bed.

"Enough," Morgan roared. The room fell silent. "You cannot hide any longer, Isla. It is time to pay. I warned you, but you didn't listen. Human and fae do not mix."

I pulled on my magic again, debating what to do. I could form a shield around myself, protect the baby, keep us safe.

"Your magic won't work, Isla. Give up," Morgan spat, but I ignored her.

How did they get in? How did they block the mindchat? Questions swirled. I had no answers as the three queens stood there, watching me squirm.

"Did you think you were the only one with magic?" Morgan asked. "My father prepared for this. After Sheba, he swore fae and humans would never again unite. The most powerful sorcerers are in his control. They allowed us to break through your shield. You cannot win, Isla."

Blue light began to pulse around me.

"You can shield yourself if you like, pull all your magic to you, but I wouldn't if I were you," Iona, the Winter queen, smirked.

"And why is that?" I sneered.

The queens looked at one another and smiled. "My men surround your beloved human. One word from me and… Well, you know," she said, running her finger across her throat, as if it were a knife.

"You can't kill Sean," I shouted. "If he dies, I die, then you don't get your revenge."

"Oh, we're not going to kill him," Morgan said. "Father has means of keeping him intact until we're finished with you and that…abomination."

My body tensed. My daughter. They were after my daughter. "What do you want?" I screamed at Morgan.

"Justice. You violated our laws, Isla. You must be punished."

"You won't take me alive," I screamed. "My daughter will be born. She will live and destroy your lies."

As if hearing my words, the contractions started again. Worse this time. I fought to catch my breath. I wanted to push. "No… Please, no," I sobbed as my body began to take over. "You can't come yet. Your dad's not here."

I didn't want to do this on my own. I didn't want Sean to miss the moment our daughter came into the world. It was the one thing we'd been fighting for this past year, and now, because of them, he wasn't here.

A darkness swept through my body as I counted my breaths. *Deep breath in, out, in, out.* When the urge became too strong, I pushed, the queens watching from the end of my bed. I tried so hard to fight it, to stop the inevitable, but it was no use. As the last contraction ripped through my body, my thoughts fell on Sean.

"I'm sorry, my love. I need to protect our daughter." I knew I would have to lower his shield, doom him.

CHAPTER SEVEN

Her small cry proclaimed their failure. My baby girl. The queens watched my every movement. As I brought her to my breast, I reveled in her perfection. She was beautiful. Soft, black curls framed her delicate face. A button nose, just like her father's. She snuggled into my breast, and I lowered my face to take in her scent. A new baby smell was like no other. I stroked her cheek, her soft curls.

We've done it, Sean, I whispered in my mind, hoping he felt the joy coursing through my veins.

The queens mumbled to each other again, but I ignored them. They were too late. My daughter was here and she was perfect. I lowered my lips to kiss her forehead, feeling her warm skin, her little fingers gripped around mine. My heart filled with love for this tiny being in my arms. It was a feeling unlike anything I'd ever felt before. I was connected to her in a way more powerful than any magic, and I felt whole as this little life snuggled to me.

Sean may have missed her birth, but I would save him.

Memories of our time together flooded my mind. Our first kiss, our declarations of love, and the punishment that followed. I thought of May and all she had given us, too.

Without warning, the air in my cabin turned icy.

"We warned you there would be consequences. There can be no half-breeds," Morgan and the queens said.

I looked up. My heart stuttered as ice began to form along the hairs of my arms. My gaze fell back to my daughter. She'd stopped moving, her eyes closed. Her tiny fingers no longer gripped mine. Something was wrong. Terror filled me as I watched her pink skin lose its color. I shook her gently, rubbing my face against hers to create warmth. Nothing worked. Black veins emerged as her skin began to lighten and become translucent. I cuddled her tighter, closer to my breast. She needed warmth, that was all. I pulled on my magic, coating her in blue light. It was no use. Nothing happened. My tears fell upon her as her skin began to disintegrate. Each one like acid, tearing her apart. Her muscles deteriorated before my eyes. I struggled to cling to the skeletal figure that remained. I cast spell after spell, shouting the words into the darkness, but they fell on deaf ears. Her bones turned to dust in my arms. My beautiful baby girl vanished. The only reminder was the lingering scent of new baby and the ashes in my hands.

Where was she? What had they done with her?

I looked around in desperation. They had hidden her from me. It was a trick. She wasn't really gone. My mind snapped. I tilted my head toward the goddesses, my screams filling the air. A scream of destruction heard the world over.

"We told you there'd be consequences. Half-breeds are

an abomination. We cannot allow them."

"*You*!" I screamed. "*You* cannot allow them. What have you done with my daughter?" I clenched my fists and pulled all my magic toward me. "You will pay," I screamed. "You will bring my daughter back."

I felt the rage inside grow, and black tendrils leaked from my fingertips. Morgan and the others moved back, their eyes widening as the air around me rippled. They nodded to each other and their bodies began to fade.

"No," I screamed, shooting lightning toward them. "You will stay."

Words flowed from my mouth in a rare, ancient language.

"Isla, no! You mustn't!"

"Do not speak to me!" my voice echoed as the power raged inside me. "You will bring my daughter back or face my wrath."

"We cannot. It is the will of the universe. Fae and humans cannot mix. It is not done."

"It *was* done! Bring her back or you will die."

"We cannot die, Isla. Let us help you. Let us remove your pain. Come home with us now."

"Never." I raised my hands, allowing all the magic to take over my body. "You will pay. You will suffer as I have."

My lips curled as I released my power on them. They tried to retreat, transport themselves back to wherever they came from, only to be flung back into my cabin. The magic coursing through my veins held them in place.

"Will you return my daughter?"

"We cannot," they cried, fear present in their eyes for

the first time.

The all-powerful queens cowered before me. They realized what was to come and begged for mercy.

"Then so be it. You shall be no more!" I shrieked.

I smiled as black veins appeared on their faces, their skin slowly disintegrating. I laughed as their agonizing screams echoed around the small cabin. Their bones turned to ash and they were no more. They suffered, just as I had.

As their ashes coated the floor of the cabin, my body slumped back, drained. I was alone. The shield evaporated, no magic remained. I relived my daughter's birth repeatedly. I memorized her smell, her dark curls, every little detail as my wailing filled the night.

In the early hours of the morning, numbness replaced my pain and swallowed my grief, trapping it deep inside. I would no longer cry. I would have my revenge. I thought of Sean as sleep took me.

***

I woke with a start, my surroundings dark. My hands were bound behind my back.

"Isla, you have destroyed your own. You must be punished."

I looked up. Morgan's father, king of the Summer Court, stood in front of me. "Do your worst," I spat. "They deserved it. I will curse the lot of you."

"You took fae lives, used magic to destroy. You will be banished forever. You will become the messenger of death until the day you beg for my forgiveness."

"I will *never* beg for your forgiveness. They took

everything from me. They deserved to die. I will not show remorse."

"So be it. You are hereby sentenced to an eternity of banishment. You will roam the human world you chose to love, never to be granted peace. You will herald pain and death for those you chose above your own. You will not exist to them. You will watch forever as life passes by."

"Do your worst," I screamed.

In an instant, I found myself back in the cabin, safe in bed. Everything looked just as I had left it.

Sean crashed through the door shortly after, calling my name. I tried to reach out to him, call his name, but it was useless. He could not see or hear me. I slumped to the floor in the corner of the cabin and wept.

My runes were still intact, the bond still there, but I had no magic, no power. I existed in silence, just as Morgan's father had promised. A silent watcher.

Sean left the cabin, but I could not follow. I was trapped here. I heard him calling my name, searching for clues, anything. He returned later that evening and sat by the fire. He put his head in his hands and wept.

I tried everything I could to communicate with him. Nothing worked. I watched, invisible, as he drove himself mad. He repeated his actions day after day. I expected him to give up, to move on with his life, but he didn't.

I spent my days trying to summon my magic, recalling all I had read in May's books. I remembered her warning. Had I destroyed my magic when I killed Morgan and the other queens? My intention had been to destroy. They deserved it, and I wasn't sorry. I would do it again if I had to. I remembered the black tendrils of energy I had summoned, too. Was it still there inside me?

The final stage of my punishment, my curse, came without warning. As Sean drowned his sorrows in a bottle of whiskey, I paced the cabin, trying to reach out to him. Suddenly, a searing pain ripped through my stomach. I reached down and felt my swollen belly. My baby was back.

"Sean, look! She's back. She's coming," I shouted.

He didn't move.

I went through it all again—the contractions, the pain, the pushing, giving birth.

"Sean, look!" I said, holding her close as tears spilled from my eyes.

She was here, my beautiful baby girl. I held her, smelled her soft skin, and ran my hand over her black curls. The air turned cold. Just like before, I watched as my precious baby turned to dust in my arms.

My tortured screams filled the air. Sean dropped the bottle of whiskey on the floor. He heard me. He called my name in terror as he jumped up, searching for me. I vanished, reappearing somewhere in the village. My screams sounded through the night, lasting for three days as my daughter came into the world and disappeared twice more.

My labor and the birth of my daughter repeated. Finally, I made the connection between it and the curse. Morgan's father had cursed me to feel my daughter's birth and death over and over again, but it always coincided with the death of one of Sean's loved ones. The first time was his father. Sean had followed my cries and been there when he passed away. The second time was his mother. By the third time, Sean realized the sound of my wailing was tied to the death of someone he loved. This time, it was his youngest niece. A fever had taken her body, and as my daughter disappeared on the third night, so did this young girl's life. I had become his own personal messenger of death.

CHAPTER EIGHT

The years passed in silence, Sean remaining by my side as I watched him age, his determination never waning.

"I will find you, Isla," he whispered as he sat by the fire each evening. "I will find the truth."

More than anything, I wished I could alleviate his pain, show him what had become of me. The fae never entered the human world again, no mating bond ever formed. It was as if they had disappeared. Only Sean and I remained, our bond still intact. I tried to find my magic, tried to end the curse, but nothing worked. In the end, I gave in to despair, gave in to the darkness that shrouded me, and slept. I woke only when death was near and cried for those who would soon greet it. For three nights, I gave birth and watched my daughter disintegrate in my arms.

For three nights, grief consumed me. I travelled the island of Ireland. Many saw me, my long hair blowing in the breeze, but it was my wailing, my heart breaking in two as my daughter was ripped away, that was acknowledged.

I slept only to wake to grief. As the years passed, it wasn't revenge I sought anymore, but peace. I craved silence. I craved an end to my torture. All I had to do was call out for forgiveness. Give Morgan's father what he wanted. I couldn't do it, though. It would be a lie. I held no remorse for Morgan or the queens whose lives I took. They deserved it.

I woke late one winter's eve, snow thick on the ground. Sean lay in bed, his hair now grey, his face wrinkled. I screamed as pain ripped through my body. I saw him tremble. His eyes fluttered open and he turned to face me.

"Isla, is that you, mo chroí?"

"Sean," I whispered, knowing that I would disappear any moment.

"I hear you," he said, struggling to sit up. His head turned in my direction as he wiped the sleep from his eyes. "Isla, it *is* you."

"You see me?" I gasped.

"Yes, mo chroí. I see you," he said through his tears. "You're really here."

"I've always been here, Sean. I've always been with you."

"Come closer."

I moved toward him, holding my breath. "I don't know how long I have, Sean. I'm sorry."

"Come, sit beside me. Let me look at you. I've missed you so much."

"I know," I sobbed, sitting on the bed beside him.

Another pain shot through me. It was happening again.

Sean's eyes widened. "The baby?"

"Yes," I said, bowing my head. "I'm sorry, Sean. I couldn't stop them. I couldn't save her."

"Isla, tell me what happened that day. Tell me the

truth."

I raised my head, my eyes meeting his. I told him what Morgan had done to our daughter, then what her father had done to me. I told him as much as I could before the pain became too great.

"I have to leave, Sean, before it's too late. You can't see this. You can't," I cried as I gripped my stomach.

Sean reached for my hand. "Stay, Isla, please. My time is coming to an end. I want to spend my last moments with you."

That was when I realized I wouldn't be leaving. I would stay and watch, and grieve, as my mate left this world. "Sean," I sobbed as I turned away from him. "I don't want you to see what happens. I don't want you to see what they did to our daughter."

"Isla, I've felt your pain. I've heard the terror in your cries all these years. Let me find peace. Let me finally know the truth."

I turned toward him, tears streaming down my face as I nodded. I would give him what I craved. I would give him peace.

Our daughter was born as my cries pierced the night. Her tiny body cradled in my hands, I couldn't look at her. I couldn't bring myself to gaze upon her dark curls, smell the newborn scent that wafted off her. I knew what was to come as I looked away, her body going stiff in my arms. I heard Sean gasp as I felt her slip away.

"No," he shouted. "Isla, what happened? Where is she?"

I turned to face him, my body wracked with sobs. "This is what happens. Every night for three nights, she is born, then she dies. For fifty years, I have endured this endless torture and I can't stop it. I can't make her stay. I can't do anything. I have no magic," I sobbed. "I just want it to end."

Sean reached out and stroked my arm. "We will find a way…together."

"We can't. There is no way. They cursed me, Sean. They stole our baby and cursed me to this endless torture. I've watched you day after day. I've sat here trapped in the silence, tormented by grief, wondering if today will be the day our daughter will die again."

Sean pulled me into his arms, and for the first time since that dreadful night, I felt him. I felt his arms around me. I felt his tears as they rolled onto my head. I felt his heartbeat. I felt him.

"All this time, you've been here, but I couldn't feel you." He shook his head. "What of the bond, Isla? I still have my runes."

"I don't know what they did, Sean."

We sat in silence, wrapped in each other's embrace as we waited for death to come.

After about an hour, Sean cleared his throat. "How long do I have?"

I lifted my head from his chest and looked into his blue eyes. I swallowed hard. "Two days."

"Then we have two days to break this curse."

"I've tried. It can't be done," I sighed.

"We haven't tried together, mo chroi."

I snuggled into him once more and let sleep take me.

***

When I woke the next evening, Sean was seated beside the fire, his head bowed.

"Sean," I whispered as I sat up in the bed.

"Isla." He turned toward me. "I couldn't wake you."

"That's what happens," I said, looking at the floor. "It will happen again tonight, Sean. The same thing over and over."

"Is that why you couldn't look at her?"

"Yes. I can't bear to watch it anymore. I know that sounds terrible, but I just can't, Sean. I can't watch as she stops moving, stops breathing..."

"It's okay, love. I understand," he said, turning back to the fire. "Your heart is broken, as is mine."

I sat beside him, seeing the torment on his face. "She was beautiful," I whispered. "My hair and your nose. I thought I could keep her safe. I didn't know."

Sean turned to me. "What did you do to them, Isla?"

"When they...did what they did, I pulled every ounce of magic into me and set it free upon them. I did to them what they did to our daughter."

"I see, and was this magic black?"

"Yes," I gasped. "How did you know?"

"I was coming back from the village. The shield was still intact, but something happened and I lost my way. I was surrounded by fae. They didn't attack. They just stood there, smiling at me. I didn't know what to do, so I kept walking. I heard you scream, then a black smoke surrounded my shield. When it cleared, they were all dead. Whatever magic you used, Isla, it wiped them out. My shield fell, and I found myself on the other side of the mountain. By the time I made it home, you were gone."

I took in a deep breath. "I was here when you got home. I tried to reach you, but you couldn't hear or see me. I watched you search the garden and tear the cabin apart looking for us."

"We found each other in the end," he whispered.

My contractions started again, and Sean helped me to the bed. "Please, leave me," I begged.

"No, Isla, I'm staying. This is how it should have been."

"But, Sean, you know what will happen…"

"I do."

My screams filled the air as I got ready to push. "Please, Sean. Don't look."

He gripped my hand. "Together," he said. He kissed the top of my head before moving to the end of the bed. "I can see her head. She's coming."

With one last push, our daughter came into the world. Her small cry made my heart skip.

"Hello, Aisling," Sean said, lifting her into his arms. "Aren't you beautiful…just like your mom."

I heard her cry again.

"Want to meet your mom?" Sean asked as he moved around the bed. "She's beautiful, Isla. Look." He held her out to me, but I shook my head.

"I can't," I sobbed. "I can't see her die. Not again."

Sean snuggled her close. "She's perfect, Isla, and she's smiling at me. Look." He sat on the bed beside me, holding our little girl. She wriggled in his arms. "She's got a strong grip, this one."

I remembered how her little fingers had curled around

mine. How she nuzzled into me. I heard the joy in Sean's voice and felt my heart breaking.

"Do you want to hold her?" he asked.

"More than anything," I whispered. "But I can't. Just place her beside me. It will be over in a minute."

Sean gasped. "You can't mean that, Isla. You can't let her suffer alone. I'll hold her. Just tell me what to do."

"There's nothing you can do," I sobbed. "She turns cold, stops moving, and…"

I reached out my hand and pulled it back again.

"Here," Sean said, taking my hand in his. "We'll do it together."

He linked his fingers with mine, our runes touching, and brought our hands to our daughter's head. I felt her soft curls on my fingertips as tears slipped from my eyes. "Aisling," I sobbed. "My beautiful baby girl."

I heard Sean take a deep breath, and I held my own. This was it. It was happening.

"Isla, you're glowing. Open your eyes."

I snapped my eyes open. He was right. My runes were glowing blue, a soft light spreading out from our hands. My magic had returned. I sat up. "Is she…?"

"Still breathing, and smiling," Sean said.

"Let me see." I lifted my hands into the air, my magic pulsing.

When he leaned over, I saw her rosy cheeks. She was smiling. She was alive.

"How?" I spluttered, reaching out for her.

Sean placed her into my arms and my magic surrounded her. She closed her eyes, panic rose inside me. "Sean?"

"It's okay, love. She's sleeping. Look. Her chest is moving. She's alive, Isla."

I pulled her into my chest and inhaled deeply as she nuzzled closer, her little eyes fluttering. "She's still here," I sobbed. For the first time in fifty years, I allowed joy to fill me, hope to rise. I smiled.

Sean sat beside me. "We did it...together," he whispered.

"We did," I said, looking up at him.

His face scrunched in pain.

"What is it?" I asked. "What's wrong, Sean?"

He held his hand up. His rune glowed, a blue light coming from it. It formed around his whole body before disintegrating.

My hand flew to my mouth. "Sean, you're young again."

He lifted his hand and looked at it, shock on his face. "What's happening?"

"Let me be the one to answer that," a voice said from the cabin door.

We both turned. "May?" I gasped.

"Yes, Isla, it's me. You've done well, my child."

"I don't understand. You died, May. How are you here?"

"You broke the darkness of your curse. You are now free."

"And Sean? My daughter? What happens to them? Sean is dying, his time is almost here."

May nodded. "You freed them, too, Isla. But there is something else."

"What?"

"In breaking the curse and defeating the darkness, you ended your life."

I sucked in a breath. "I'm dead?"

"In a way, yes. You are in the afterlife, but don't worry. It's not a bad thing. You get to be with Sean and your child. You get to have the life that was stolen from you."

"But how?"

"Love." May smiled. "Your bond with Sean was stronger than anything else. When you allowed him to take your daughter, to see the truth, you opened the way to break the curse. He gave her the love you had been forced to withhold. In trusting him, in joining hands and touching her together, you broke the darkness. Nothing is stronger than love, Isla. Nothing."

"But what of the curse, May? Is it truly broken?"

She lowered her head. "Not entirely. You cannot undo everything. You get to remain in the afterlife with Sean and your child, but you must still warn the humans of impending death."

"So, I'm still cursed?"

"It is what you choose to see it as," May said, then disappeared.

I looked at Sean, then down at the little bundle asleep in my arms. "We won," I whispered. "We did it together."

"We did, love." He kissed the top of my forehead. "We always will."

"But what of the curse?" I asked.

"Maybe it's not a curse anymore," Sean said, scratching his chin. "What did May say? It depends on how you see it."

"What other way is there to see it? I bring pain and

death, suffering and grief."

"You aren't the one who brings it, Isla. Death is inevitable. You don't kill people. You warn them of what is to come. Perhaps it's not a curse at all."

I looked at him, his words sinking in. He was right. What I conceived as a curse was perhaps also a gift. In that moment, I realized I could bring a gift.

"What is it?" Sean asked.

"I've been given a gift." His brow furrowed. "Don't you see? My cries of pain are a gift. The gift of goodbye, of treasured last moments. Moments that will remain in their memories for years to come. Time is precious. With my gift, I can remind people of this."

Sean smiled. "You, Isla, are my gift. Even if all I had been given was a day with you, it would have been the best day of my life."

"It's good we broke the curse," I said. "If we hadn't, we would only have had three days together before I would have had to say goodbye."

"Three days can be a lifetime if you spend it wisely. You will give this gift to the world, Isla. The gift of time."

I smiled at the man I loved with all my heart. We now had all the time we wanted.

EPILOGUE

As time passed, I began to sense death and would leave the afterlife. For three nights, my keening would be heard by the family of the person death intended to visit. My wailing warned of what was to come. People recognized the importance of my cries. They gave me the name of Banshee, messenger of death. They listened to my warnings. Will you?

When you hear me, death is near, but it is not a curse. It is a gift. The gift of goodbye. The chance to say all that remains in your heart. The chance to spend final moments with your loved ones. The chance to create everlasting memories. Heed me well. Time is precious. Use it wisely. Find joy in your days, and love with all your heart. Remember, death comes for you all, so live every moment and treasure the gift of time. You never know when the sand will run out.

The End

If you enjoyed reading Hear Me Cry, I'd love if you could leave a review. It doesn't have to be long, a couple of words is all that's required. Reviews really do help authors and other readers find books.

ABOUT THE AUTHOR

I am a freelance writer, poet, and author. I live in Co. Meath, Ireland with my husband and two children. I am known locally by my married name, Donnelly, but I write under my maiden name of Evans. My writing was published in several magazines and journals in 2016 and 2017. I am also the author of *Surviving Suicide: A Memoir from Those Death Left Behind,* published in 2012. When I'm not writing for work clients, I am usually reading the latest novels from some of the amazing indie authors out there, or sharing snippets from my latest manuscripts with my husband and children.

I've always loved writing. My passion began at a very young age and I wrote my first book at the age of 9. Writing my first full-length novella, Finding Forever, was my first step into the fiction publishing world and while I was nervous, I was also very excited. This has been my dream for so long and to finally have the courage to pen stories and publish them is something I always wanted to do.

Finding Forever began as a prompt from my writers' group. Our prompt was "pirates" and I wrote the first 1,000 words ending where Liz finds herself on the pirate ship. It sat idle on my laptop for almost a year before I picked it up again. I was doing a page a day challenge and decided that for the month I would work on finishing some of the pieces in my "to be completed" file on my computer. Little did I know when I picked up my pen to work on this that it would turn into a novella. The twists and turns that Finding Forever takes were a total surprise to me. I hadn't planned the story. I never dreamed it would be any more than a short story. The moment when I wrote about cameras, I knew something wonderful was about to happen. When I write, I allow the characters to tell me their story. I don't plan things out. I just let the story tell itself. I was so pleased with the initial beta reader response to this story which encouraged me to publish. In July 2017, I discovered that Finding Forever had made the list of 98 Best Books of 2017 according to Goodreads users and it won the 2017 Summer Indie Book Award for Best Thriller.

Save Her Soul, began in the same way. I had finished writing Finding Forever and just picked up my pen and started writing something new. I had no idea what the story was going to be about, but once I started writing that first chapter with Kate and then that sleaze Tidsdale, I knew I was going to fall in love with the characters. I believed that Drake would be an evil demon as I began writing his character and I was probably as surprised as you were when his character began to change. I really enjoyed writing this story and love how it ended perfectly. Save Her Soul won the Silver Award for Best Paranormal in the Virtual Fantasy Con 2017.

Hear Me Cry was originally written as a short story just over 2,000 words, for the Irish IMBAS Celtic Mythology Competition in 2017. It didn't win and had been sitting on my computer. When I saw a call for a Myths and Legends anthology, I thought my story would be perfect and applied. I was thrilled to be accepted and later discovered that the minimum word count was 20,000. I then had to turn my short story into the novella that Hear Me Cry is today. It wasn't easy, especially not as a pantser and I ended up with 25K words of a completely different novel before Hear Me Cry was born. I really wanted to do something different and instead of focusing on the usual horror themes that surround the Banshee, I went for something completely different. I hope you've enjoyed my interpretation of the book and if you have any questions, I'm always more than happy to answer them.

I also secured a two-book publishing deal with Handersen Publishing in 2017. They are a children's book publisher based in Nebraska. The first book, Nightmare Realities, was published on the 25th September 2017, and is a collection of spooky stories. The second book is a middle grade novel, that I am currently working on.

If you'd like to keep up to date with what I'm working on, you can find more information on my website: http://www.amandajevans.com and on Facebook: http://www.facebook.com/amandajevanswriter.

Sign up for my newsletter for sneak peaks of upcoming books, cover reveals, and more.
http://eepurl.com/cz3cfr

Finding Forever

A Romantic Suspense Novella

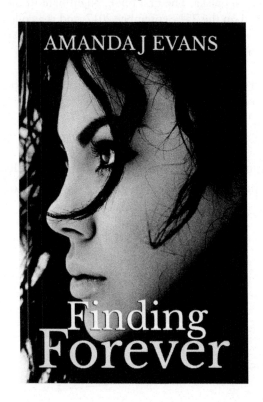

When Love Refuses To Give Up

I look at his face, the face of the man who holds my heart, my forever. But his heart has stopped beating.

A Woman desperately searching for her forever…

Liz Parker thought she'd found her forever the moment she said, "I do", but fate had other ideas. Waking up with a tattered wedding dress and her dead husband in her arms was not the way she planned her honeymoon. Distraught, all she wants to do is die along with him. Instead she is unexpectedly rescued, but Charles' body is left behind. She is determined to go back and recover her husband's body and give him a proper burial.

Two lives collide…

When Liz meets John, he becomes her only hope, her chance to bring Charles' body home, but there's something more. Why does he look at her with such pity? Why does he agree to help her, when no one else will? Why won't anyone believe that Charles exists?

All is not what it seems. An enemy from the past, intent on revenge, hasn't finished what he started. Liz must find out the truth about the accident and what really happened to her husband. She'll put her life at risk in order to find and keep love forever.

Finding Forever the debut novella from Amanda J Evans. A blend of psychological thriller mixed with romance and unexpected twists. Finding Forever will prove to you that when you believe in love, anything is possible.

Praise for Finding Forever:

"Really enjoyed it…didn't want to go to bed without finishing

it....brilliant" Maria B Bourke

"I really enjoyed it. The suspense kept me reading to the end." Lesley Robson

"Fantastic story! Kept me gripped from the beginning. The twists were amazing." Sarah Ellis

"Absolutely brilliant. It was great. Action, intrigue, and romance all rolled into one neat tidy package." Terri Osborn

Available Now in e-book and paperback

Save Her Soul

A Paranormal Romance

What would you be willing to give up to get your revenge?

Kate is willing to give up everything to see her sister's murderer get what he deserves. She's gathered evidence. She's learned to fight, and now she's ready for payback.

Revenge is her reason for living and all she thinks about is watching the killer's face as the last breath leaves his body.

Drake's no ordinary guy. For centuries, he's been trying to save Kate's soul. His mission - to make sure the evil trapped insider her is never released. But time is running out. Can Drake stop Kate from unleashing hell on earth or is the world doomed?

Their fates are tied in more ways than they realize and as secrets are revealed, Drake is put to the ultimate test. Can he find the strength needed to break the curse? Will Kate finally get her revenge and unknowingly unleash the ancient evil hidden within her?

Find out in this new paranormal romance from Amanda J Evans

Praise for Save Her Soul

"Dark Paranormal that gets it right. A story that will keep you turning the pages"

"Mystery, romance, and action all in one fantastic story"

"Dark paranormal, love is endless"

"Love, revenge, death, rebirth, curses, star-crossed lovers – the storyline of Save Her Soul is original with its unexpected twists and turns."

Available Now in ebook and paperback

Printed in Great Britain
by Amazon